Hazel's Heart

The Willoughby Witches

(Book Two)
by
Terri Reid

Hazel's Heart

The Willoughby Witches

(Book Two)

by Terri Reid

The author would like to thank all those who have contributed to the creation of this book: Richard Reid, Sarah Reid, Peggy Hannah, Mickey Claus, Terrie Snyder, and Hillary Gadd. And especially to the wonderful readers who are starting this whole new adventure with me, thank you all!

Chapter One

Hazel Willoughby pulled her bright red pick-up truck behind the feed store in Whitewater, Wisconsin. She glanced at the parking spot right next to the loading block and frowned when she discovered it was already taken.

"Don't they know I needed that spot?" she muttered, sliding her sunglasses down from her large, hazel-brown eyes and pushing her long, chestnut hair back over her shoulders. She   contemplated her list that included several fifty-pound sacks of goat feed, as well as sacks of grain and milk replacer. She looked at the minivan thoughtfully. Would they really remember that they parked next to the loading block? she wondered. With just a quick wave of her hand she could magically move the minivan down two spots. She sighed and shook her head. She could hear her mother's voice in her mind reminding her that they needed to keep a low profile and refrain from any extemporaneous spells.

"Remember, Hazel," Agnes Willoughby's voice echoed in her brain. "Things are changing, and we need to be very wise about how we use our abilities."

"How does she get into my mind like that?" she sighed, rolling her eyes, and then she turned the steering wheel and headed to the empty spot two car widths away.

She opened the door of the pickup, grabbed her purse, stepped onto the running board and then hopped down to the ground. The height of the four-wheel drive pick-up with studded off-road tires had always been a slight problem for Hazel's five-feet four-inch stature, but the running board and a little bit of a hop to the ground, made it manageable.

She walked around to the side door and entered the store. She paused, for just a moment, to inhale the familiar scents of her favorite store. The sweet scent of dried molasses from the feed mix coupled with the fragrance of dried corn and oats created a warm undertone. The rubber from the large tractor tires displayed in a far corner added an acrid note to the mix.

2

And the cedar wood chips for bedding material released a musky aroma that pulled it all together. To Hazel, it was the scent of belonging and accomplishment, and there was nothing more appealing than that.

With her list in hand, she headed toward the customer service counter in the back of the store. It wasn't until she placed her list down on the old, worn and scarred wooden counter that she noticed the sudden shift in the atmosphere of the store. She looked over her shoulder and saw several people exiting quickly through the front door. She peered through the display windows to see if she'd missed a threatening storm system heading their way, but the day remained bright and sunny.

The hairs on the back of her neck began to rise and she quickly turned the other way to see a tall, blonde woman dressed in black leather pants and jacket approach her. The clothing looked like she had been poured into it and the jacket was zipped low enough to ensure her charms were on display to the whole world.

"Wanda," Hazel said with a terse nod and then turned back towards the counter.

"Don't turn your back on me," Wanda spat, coming up alongside Hazel.

Hazel shrugged and sent a careless glance over her shoulder. "Sorry, is there something you need?"

"You Willoughbys think you're better than everyone," Wanda hissed. "Well, we're going to show you. We're going to show you good."

Hazel nodded slowly. "Okay, then," she said, with a shrug. "Are we done now? I really have work to do."

Wanda's eyes widened in rage and her face turned red. "We are not done. Not by a long-shot. I know what you did to my father," she growled.

Hazel met Wanda's eyes steadily. "That's right," she replied evenly. "How's he doing?" she paused for a moment, feigning recall. "That's right, he's up in Iron Mountain prison, isn't he?" She shook her head. "I was surprised to hear that he was involved in drug dealing."

4

Wanda raised her hand and swung it to slap Hazel, but Hazel grabbed her arm and held it inches from her face. Suddenly, Hazel's eyes brightened, and her hair floated softly around her face, as if moved by a light breeze. The store smelled as if it had been filled with electricity, like the air after a thunderstorm, supercharged with nitrogen.

"You don't want to do that," Hazel said, her voice surprisingly mild.

Wanda sputtered, the anger replaced by fear and tried to pull her arm away, but Hazel held it tightly for another long moment and then, finally, released it.

Wanda tottered backwards. "This is not the end of this," she whispered, her throat tight. "We are going to win this time. We're going to have the power this time. I've seen what the Master has in store for you and your family." She laughed bitterly. "We'll see how cute you are when you're locked in your own prison."

A chill went down Hazel's spine, but she kept her eyes calm and her voice steady. "Dramatic much, Wanda," she said, rolling her eyes.

Skewering Hazel with a malevolent glare, Wanda finally turned and marched out of the store.

Once the door closed, Hazel closed her eyes and released a slow, steady breath.

"You okay there?" Harley, the store owner, asked.

Hazel opened her eyes, looked up at the tall, old man with gentle blue eyes and pure white hair, and smiled. "I'm good, thanks Harley," she said.

Harley looked past her at the empty store and then met her eyes, now the kindness was replaced with concern. "I'm wondering if it might not be better for you to call in your order," he said softly. "I'll give you free delivery."

"Why?" she asked, confused.

He shook his head sadly. "Folks been talking about strange things happening around town," he said.

"Talk of coven wars and evil spells. Got most regular people pretty spooked."

"And they blame us," Hazel said with a slow nod. Her heart sank, and she felt tears wet her eyes. "But it's not us, Harley. We're not the bad guys."

He shrugged and sighed. "Don't matter what the truth is," he said. "What matters is what people think, 'specially if you got a store to run and products to sell."

"So, I'm chasing away your customers," she replied. "Just by walking in the door."

"Yeah, seems like," he said. "I wish I were a stronger man and I could say to hell with them, you just come and go as you please. But I can't, Hazel. I need those customers."

"Well, you shouldn't be put out of business because of me," she replied, and she slid the list over to him. "This is what I need today. Should I wait for it, or do you want to deliver."

Harley looked up and saw people standing outside the store peering in. "We'll deliver," he said, closing his eyes in regret and shaking his head.

When he opened his eyes, Hazel could see his remorse and placed her hand over his. "It's okay, Harley," she said softly. "I understand."

Chapter Two

Pulling the door closed behind her, Hazel searched through her purse for her keys. Automatically walking toward her park car, as she rifled through the bottom of her purse, she didn't glance up until she had keys in hand. And, to her great surprise, her truck wasn't there.

Confused, she glanced around the parking lot. No, she didn't park it somewhere else, there were no bright red pickup trucks to be seen. She looked at the parking slot, it was definitely not handicapped parking, so she couldn't have been towed. Someone had stolen her car!

She pulled her phone out of her purse and started to call 9-1-1, when she glanced toward the road. She could see the tail end of a police car parked in front of the store. Stashing her phone in her purse, she jogged towards the police car and then stopped, in shock, as she watched a tall, police officer put a ticket on the windshield of her pickup truck.

9

"Wait," she called, rushing forward.

The tall man turned, and, for a moment, Hazel was speechless. She had realized he was tall when he was bending over the hood of her truck, but when he stood she realized he was at least six-feet, five-inches tall and he was built like a weight-lifter, his biceps stretching the material of his uniform. His dark brown hair was longer than regulation and swept nearly to his collar and his face was covered with a trimmed goatee and moustache that was as dark as his hair. His skin had an olive tone, with a strong aquiline nose. But none of those very masculine features had stopped her in her tracks as had his eyes. They were amber and slightly almond shaped, with a dark outline around the iris. They seemed almost feral, especially with thick eyebrows that angled sharply above them, and those eyes were pointedly focused on her.

"May I help you?" he asked, his deep voice breaking her out of her stupor.

She shook her head slightly and then nodded. "Yes. Yes, you can," she replied. "This is my truck…"

10

"Do you often park in front of a fire hydrant?" he asked, one of those angled brows raising on his forehead.

"No. No, I don't," she said, then shook her head again. "I mean, I never do. I never park in front of a fire hydrant."

He glanced down at her truck and then gazed at her.

"I know what this looks like," she said, waving her hands to emphasize her agitation. "But I was just coming out here to report my pickup truck stolen."

He studied her for a long moment, nodding slowly. "So, you want me to believe that someone stole your pickup truck and then parked it in front of the fire hydrant?" he asked. "And you just happen to figure that out as I was writing you a ticket?"

"Yes," she said emphatically and then she shook her head. "I mean, no. That's not just what I want you to believe. It's the truth. I parked behind the store. I always park behind the store because my order is always so big.

But when I left the store, my pickup was gone. And I was about to call the police, when I saw your car."

"Where's your order?" he asked.

She opened her mouth, closed it and then sighed. "It's being delivered," she said softly. "But really, just watch any of the closed-circuit cameras in the area. They'll prove that I'm..."

"Lady, I don't have time to watch cameras," he said. "Your pickup was parked illegally. You're getting a ticket."

He reached over, pulled the ticket from behind the windshield wiper and handed it to her personally. "And next time, get a better story," he said.

Frustration and anger bubbled over as Hazel ripped the ticket from his hand. "Listen, buddy," she seethed. "I have had a really bad day already and I don't need some smart-ass cop giving me a hard time just because he's too lazy to look at the evidence to prove my case. I want your name. I'm going to file a complaint with your police chief."

A wisp of a smile played across his face, but then it disappeared as quickly as it had come. "Yes, ma'am," he said with a slightly sardonic nod. "My name is Joseph Norwalk. It's right there on the ticket, next to arresting officer."

She glanced down, and her heart sank. "Chief Joseph Norwalk," she read softly.

This time he allowed the smile to stay. "You have a nice day, ma'am."

Chapter Three

Agnes Willoughby looked up from her baking, a frown appearing on her otherwise pleasant face. At nearly fifty, the mother of three adult daughters was often confused as their sister with her trim shape, sparkling green eyes and shoulder-length auburn hair. She wiped her flour-covered hands on a dishtowel, pulled her apron over her head, tossed it on the nearest kitchen chair and headed to the back door.

Hurrying onto the back deck, she spied her daughter, Rowan, and Henry McDermott, Rowan's fiancé, jogging across the backyard towards the barn. Rowan's bright red hair was loose around her shoulders and Agnes was grateful to see that her middle-child no longer wore oversized glasses on her face, to hide her beauty. And the look that passed between Rowan and Henry warmed Agnes' heart. They were completely and utterly in love.

Rowan glanced over and smiled at her mother. "So, you felt it too?" she asked.

Agnes nodded and hurried down the stairs to join them, her long cotton skirt held up with one hand. "Something has Hazel riled up," she agreed. "And a riled-up Hazel can be dangerous."

Henry looked at Rowan. "How dangerous?" he asked, his British accent tempered with a little bit of a Midwestern twang.

She shook her head and her face was somber, but her eyes still held a twinkle in them. "You don't want to know," she said.

"Because then you would have to kill me?" Henry jested.

She smiled. "If Hazel hadn't already done it," she replied.

"Wow! Okay," he said. "Serious."

They stopped at the edge of the driveway nearest to the barn where Hazel raised and coddled a herd of dairy goats. "She'll come here first," Agnes said, walking up alongside them. "The goats always calm her."

"Then shouldn't we just let her have some time with the goats first?" Henry asked.

"Normally, yes," Agnes replied. "But with things the way they are right now, I think we need to find out if this is related to the curse."

Rowan closed her eyes for a moment and concentrated. "She's about a mile away," she said, once she'd opened her eyes. "And she's as upset as ever."

They all turned when they heard the sound of a motorized vehicle coming from the opposite direction. Catalpa Willoughby, the oldest of the three sisters, was driving their Gator across the lawn at full-speed. Cat's curly, black hair was flying behind her in the wind and her tailored blouse and slacks looked out of place on the farm equipment. Her cafe au lait skin was already sprinkled with darker freckles from too much exposure to the sun and not enough sunscreen.

She parked next to them, turned the ATV off, hopped off and joined them. "Sorry I'm late," she said. "I was working with a customer and I couldn't get away until she was done."

"You're not late," Agnes said. "She's not here yet."

"Any idea what's going on?" Cat asked.

"We're going to find out in a moment," Rowan replied as a grey plume of dust appeared down the road.

"We might want to step back," Henry suggested. "At her current rate of velocity, she might not be able to stop as quickly as she'd like."

Just as the words were out of his mouth, Hazel's red pickup careened onto the driveway and headed in their direction. Quickly taking Henry's advice, the foursome jumped back off the driveway and onto the lawn adjacent to the barn. However, Henry had underestimated Hazel's skills and the truck stopped precisely in front of the barn. The door opened and closed with a bang, and Hazel strode around the front of the truck to face them.

"What?" she demanded shortly.

"We all felt your distress several miles away,"
Agnes explained. "And we wanted to be sure that you
okay."

Hazel sighed and leaned back against the truck.
"My day has pretty much sucked and then I got a ticket,"
she said. "And I didn't even deserve it."

"I'm so sorry," Rowan said, immediately stepping
forward to hug her younger sister. "What happened?"

"Well, it seems that the whole town is talking
about a coven war," Hazel explained with a glint of anger
in her voice. "And since we are the best-known witches in
the area, suddenly we are frightening."

"Frightening?" Agnes asked, astonished. "What
have we ever done that would frighten anyone?"

Hazel shook her head. "Nothing," she said.
"Absolutely nothing. But when I walked into Harley's
Feed Store, I was not only accosted by Wanda Wildes, but
as soon as I walked in, a bunch of other customers walked
out."

Cat stepped up and nodded. "Yes, I've noticed a sudden decrease in clients at the shop," she added. "Most of the locals are staying away, my main business has been tourists."

"That's ridiculous," Henry exclaimed, angrily. "Do these people realize what you've done for them? What you've sacrificed for their safety? What this town would be like if you all just walked away and let them deal with this curse on their own?"

Hazel sighed, her eyes moist and shrugged. "No, they don't, Henry," she said. "And I don't really know if it would make a difference if they did. We're different, so we need to be feared."

"That's a complete load of bollocks!" Henry growled.

"Wow, professor," Hazel replied, surprised into grinning. "I don't think I've ever seen you this riled up before."

Henry blushed and took a deep breath. "It's not a laughing matter," he said soberly.

Hazel shook her head and went over to him, putting her hand on his arm. "No, it's not," she agreed. "But it's comforting to have true friends who are loyal no matter what." She turned to her mother and her sisters. "Harley asked me to call in my orders for the time being. But, bonus, he's going to give me free delivery."

"What?" Rowan asked. "We have always been one of Harley's best customers. What the hell?"

Hazel shrugged again. "Yeah, well, when you scare away the other clients, I guess Harley would rather us remain silent and invisible customers," she said.

"That's it," Cat said. "We'll find a new vendor for things we get from Harley. We can go to Madison or Milwaukee and get the exact same products."

"No, I want to stay with Harley," Hazel said. "He's just looking out for his business and the people who work for him. I wish he would have been more loyal. Actually, he said he wished he could be more loyal. But it is what it is."

"What happened with Wanda?" Agnes asked.

20

Hazel met her mother's eyes. "She's pretty angry about her dad and the whole prison thing," she began.

"Then maybe they shouldn't have tried to kill us," Cat said sardonically.

Hazel nodded. "She said that she's seen what the Master has in store for us. And she said that we were going to be locked in our own prison."

"He's got to win first," Rowan said. "And I am not even considering that we are going to fail. I have too much to look forward to, to even contemplate that."

Henry lifted her hand and placed a kiss on it. "I agree entirely," he said softly to Rowan.

Hazel smiled at them. "You're right. We have everything on our side," she agreed. "Doesn't good always conquer evil?"

Agnes nodded. "In all the best stories it does," she agreed.

"Oh, and finally, I can't prove it, but I think Wanda moved my truck and parked it in front of a fire hydrant," she said.

"The ticket," Cat said. "The one you didn't deserve."

"Yeah, and let's just say that I don't think the new police chief is going to be very sympathetic to our side of the cause," Hazel sighed.

Chapter Four

Chief Joseph Norwalk watched the red pickup drive down the road and sighed. Really, did people think he was that stupid? Someone stole my car and parked it illegally? She really thought he'd believe that?

Shaking his head, he moved to put his cruiser into gear when he saw Harley, the store owner, wave him over. He turned the car off, slipped out of the vehicle, and strode across the sidewalk. "Did you need something, Harley?" he asked.

"Yeah, did I see you talking with Hazel Willoughby out here?" Harley asked.

"If she owns a red pickup truck you did," Joseph replied. "Had it parked out here in front of the fire hydrant."

Harley looked down at the sidewalk, leaned back on his heels and then slowly pushed his hair back on his head. Finally, he looked up and met the policeman's eyes. "The thing is," Harley said slowly. "Hazel always parks in the back because her order's so big. I saw her come in and go out the back door myself."

"She didn't have a big order with her," Joseph countered.

"Yeah, well, that's my fault entirely," he said. "I insisted on delivering it up to her place. She would have taken it in a minute."

"She said she thought someone had taken her car and parked it here illegally, just to get her in trouble," Joseph said, watching the old man's reaction.

To his surprise, the old man didn't smile or even chuckle, just nodded slowly and ran his hand over his hair once again. "Yeah, that sounds about right," he said slowly. "That Wanda Wildes was none too happy with Hazel when she left the store. Tried to get Hazel's temper up, but Hazel's too cool of a customer for that."

Joseph smirked and shook his head. "Yeah, she didn't really seem like a cool customer when I spoke with her."

"Well, that's probably my fault," Harley admitted. "Won't say much more about that, just…I'm not proud of how I had to treat her in there."

Joseph shook his head. "So, you're saying that I should have believed her?"

"Never known a Willoughby to lie," Harley replied. "If she had parked her truck illegally, she would have admitted it and taken the ticket with no argument."

Joseph stared at Harley for a long moment, glanced up at the security camera attached to the front of the store, and then shrugged, "Those cameras up there, do they really work?"

Harley nodded. "Yes, they do," he said. "But I got to warn you, things in Whitewater aren't what you're probably used to. You got to watch those tapes with an open mind."

"Harley, I've got one of the openest minds you have ever met," Joseph answered.

"What the hell?!?" Joseph exclaimed fifteen minutes later, rewinding the tape yet another time. He was sitting in the backroom, behind the customer service desk, replaying the camera footage from just the past hour. He started with the front camera, but the tapes from the front of the store had just shown the front bumper of the pickup suddenly appearing on screen. It didn't show the windshield or the driver's area, so Joseph couldn't make a good determination on who was driving when it was parked there. Then Harley had gladly supplied the camera tapes from the back of the store.

Joseph watched Hazel park her car in the parking lot and then walk into the store. He fast-forwarded the video until he watched her leave the store, searching for her keys. Then he saw the panic on her face and saw her pull out her phone. She next looked toward the road, placed her phone in her purse and hurried toward the street.

Damn! She hadn't been lying. Someone had moved her truck!

But now, when Joseph had slowly rewound the tape to discover who had driven the truck away, all he could find was one frame where the pickup was in the parking space and the next frame it was gone.

"This can't happen," he said softly, slowing the playback down even more. "Trucks just don't unmaterialize and then rematerialize in another place."

Harley cleared his throat and Joseph turned to see the old man leaning against the doorjamb.

"There's this thing about Whitewater," Harley said slowly. "It just isn't like any town you've ever lived in."

Chapter Five

Particles of straw glistened in the sun beams that shot through the overhead windows in the barn. Hazel hefted a bushel of hay, carried it across the barn to the inside of the goat pen and dropped it into the large circular feeder. The half dozen does and their kids rushed toward the hay, eager for fresh food.

"I just fed you this morning," Hazel laughed. "Don't act like you're starving. I know better."

Brushing the pieces of hay from her work shirt, she moved around the enclosure, checking to be sure there were no breaks in the fencing that would allow predators access or conniving goats an escape route. Bending forward to inspect a spot where the steel fencing met a wooden post, she nearly toppled forward when she was gently butted on the back of her thigh. She looked over to see Lefty, the kid she, Rowan and Henry had helped deliver because his hooves had been tangled together inside his mother.

28

"Excuse me," she said, turning and sitting down on the ground in front of the baby goat. "I think I have work to do here and can't just stop and play with any goats who needs me."

Lefty pranced with delight for a moment, then quickly climbed onto Hazel's lap and settled in for a nap. Hazel's heart melted as she stroked the little goat. At most farms, the male offspring would be sold off or used for food, but even if that had been part of her production plan, she knew that Lefty would have found a permanent place on the farm, just as he had her heart. He'd been her favorite since the night he was born, and, as he softly nibbled on her work shirt, she pulled the treats she always carried for him out of her pocket.

"Hey, that's not something to eat," she complained, pulling the corner of her now wet work shirt out of his mouth. "Try these instead."

She lay her hand flat in front of his mouth and he delicately ate each small grain treat from her palm.

29

"That's a good boy," she crooned, bending over and hugging him. "You're getting so big."

His mother, now finished with her hay, bleated reproachfully at her wayward son and, his ears perked forward, he turned towards the doe.

"You really should listen to your mother," Hazel recommended. "She's just looking out for you."

The tiny goat struggled to his feet, climbed off of Hazel's lap and hopped over to stand next to his mother.

"Wise words," Agnes said, coming forward from the interior of the barn.

Hazel sat back, leaning against the fence post. "Aren't they adorable?" she asked.

Agnes smiled and nodded. "Yes, they are all adorable," she replied. "And weren't you the smart one to pick a breed that produces milk and fiber, so the little bucks don't have to be sold off."

Hazel looked up at her mom, shielding her eyes against the sun, and nodded. "How do you do that?" she asked.

"What?" Agnes asked, coming over and sitting down next to her daughter.

"Read my mind," Hazel replied.

"Well, I don't have to read your mind to see that you and Lefty have a special connection," Agnes said. "You spoil him rotten. I'm surprised that he doesn't follow you up to your room at night."

Hazel chuckled and nodded. "Yeah, well, he's like a little miracle," she explained. "And lately, I've really needed to remind myself that good things are still happening. It's not all curses and fear."

Agnes sighed. "And that's why I came out here," she said sadly. "To talk to you about what happened in town." She paused. "Would you rather I go away while you enjoy your miracle and we can talk later?"

Hazel shook her head, watching Lefty dance around his mother. "No, I think watching my miracle while we talk will be helpful," she said, then she turned to her mom. "What do you want to know."

"I want to know what frightened you," Agnes said bluntly.

Hazel nodded slowly and took the time to mentally review what had happened that morning. Finally, she inhaled deeply and replied. "I think it was the hate I felt from Wanda," she said slowly. "I've never had such deep-rooted hate hurled at me. I mean, Wanda and I were never friends, but I didn't think we were enemies. But today, when she approached me, she was my enemy and she meant me, all of us, harm. I don't understand that kind of emotion."

Agnes put her arm around her daughter and Hazel laid her head on her mother's shoulder. "No, you don't," Agnes said softly. "Because you don't hate. You protect, you love, you fight for what's right. But you don't hate. I've never seen that emotion come from you – or any of you girls."

Hazel smiled wistfully. "That's because you never taught us to hate," she said.

"Well, I hope that's true," Agnes said, stroking Hazel's long brown hair. "Because hate is an emotion that will cause more harm to the person who holds it, than to those who it is directed towards. Hate will eat you alive and will contaminate the rest of your life."

Hazel grinned. "So, what I hear you saying is that maybe I shouldn't pick up hating as a hobby?"

"You are such a brat," Agnes laughed and then sobered. "No, what you hear me saying is that I'm proud of you. I'm proud of the way you handled yourself this morning, with dignity and grace. I'm proud of the woman you have become, filled with love and light."

"Well, I don't think I was all that love and light when I dealt with the new chief of police," Hazel admitted with a sigh. "I can't imagine what he thinks of me."

Chapter Six

"What the hell am I supposed to do about this?" Joseph Norwalk asked himself as he drove down the country road, following the delivery truck from Harley's Feed Store. "I can't even believe I saw what I saw."

The delivery truck slowed and turned on its right turn signal. Joseph followed suit and was impressed by the home and the farmstead that appeared before him. He followed the truck past the house and back towards barn, parking a few yards away from the barndoor. He stepped out of his car.

"Is there something I can help you with, Chief?" Hazel asked, leaning against the deck pillar next to the stairs.

Joseph turned towards her at the sound of her voice and slowly shook his head, once again biting back a smile. For someone so little, he thought, "wait, petite, that's the word women liked, petite... Anyway, for someone so petite, she had enough attitude in her for at least couple more feet.

He nodded politely and walked towards her. Hazel felt her mouth go dry. He really is an exceptionally good-looking man, she thought and then she reminded herself, an exceptionally good man who thought I was a liar and gave me a ticket.

She walked down the stairs but stopped when she was still high enough to meet his eyes.

"I'm here to apologize," he said, standing a few feet in front of her. "And to take back the ticket I gave you."

This was not what she expected to hear coming from his mouth.

"I'm sorry. What?" she asked, astonished.

He smiled slowly and shrugged. "Yeah, well..."

Suddenly a giant black blur of fur leapt past Hazel, lips pulled back in a snarl, and charged against the police chief. The two tumbled backwards onto the grass.

"Fuzzy!" Hazel screamed as she jumped down the remaining stairs and rushed to the rescue. "Fuzzy! No!!"

But she froze in her steps when she saw the chief hold Fuzzy's head above his face and stare into his eyes. "We're good," she heard him whisper to the canine. "I'm your friend."

The snarl left the wolf's face and his long tail slowly began to wag back and forth. The Chief released his grip on Fuzzy's face and the wolf greeted him like an old friend, bathing his face in kisses. Joseph turned his face to avoid some of the licks and met Hazel's concerned and confused eyes. "Fuzzy, huh?" he asked. "Couldn't you have come up with something a little manlier?"

Her knees weak with reaction, she lowered herself to the ground and breathed out a long sigh of relief. "He never does that," she said, shaking his head. "I've never seen him do that."

Pushing the wolf off his lap, Joseph sat up and shrugged. "He perceived a threat," he said evenly. "And thought you were in danger. He's a brave and loyal friend."

She nodded slowly. How odd that he understood that Fuzzy was not a pet, but a member of the family. "Yes, he is," she replied. "But how did you get him to understand that you weren't a threat?"

Joseph smiled. "Our spirit animals communicated with each other."

"You're Native American?" Hazel asked.

He nodded. "Half," he said. "On my mother's side. My father was German."

He quickly stood up, with a nimbleness that Hazel thought would be impossible for such a large man. Then he leaned over and offered her a hand.

The minute his hand closed over hers, she felt it. Power, heat, and excitement coursed through her system as if she'd been electrified. She watched his eyes widen in surprise and knew that he had felt it too. As soon as she was on her feet, he released her hand and stepped back. She stepped back too, but the air around them was supercharged with mystical energy. They stared at each other, not speaking, trying to understand the connection that felt as old as time.

Finally, Fuzzy whined and pushed himself against Hazel. Without looking down, she laid her hand on the top of the wolf's head and slowly stroked his thick fur. Joseph nearly gasped aloud, his connection with the wolf had not broken and he could feel Hazel's gentle touch through that connection. He felt his heart accelerate and his body heat. *I need this to stop now*, he thought.

He cleared his throat loudly and took another step back. "About that ticket," he said, amazed that his voice sounded steady.

As if coming out of a daze, she shook her head, still staring at him. "I'm sorry," she whispered.

"Your ticket," he repeated, feigning impatience. "Unless, of course, you changed your mind and want to pay it."

Feeling as if she'd just been slapped, Hazel's cheeks burned. "Are you always so rude?" she asked. "Or just with women?"

I deserved that, he thought, that and a lot more.

"No, generally I have a pretty even keel," he replied, trying to appear casual. "It must be you."

Her eyes widened, and she opened her mouth to speak, then closed it tightly. She fumed for a moment, then took a deep breath. "If you'll wait here, Chief Norwalk," she said with frigid politeness. "I'll get the ticket for you."

She dashed up the steps and hurried into her home, the screen door banging shut behind her.

Fuzzy walked over to the man, leaned against him and barked softly. Looking regretfully at the door, Joseph reached down and stroked the wolf's head, mimicking Hazel's earlier actions. "It's better this way, Fuzzy," he whispered to the canine. "Much better this way."

A moment later, Hazel was back with the ticket in her hand. She handed it to him, being sure to release it

39

before they came into physical contact with each other, and then quickly stepped back.

"Thank you for your honesty," she said.

"You're being much more civil than you'd like to be," he said, studying her. "Much more civil than I deserve. Why?"

Surprised by his frankness, Hazel shook her head. "You don't know a lot about Whitewater, do you?" she asked. "And maybe that's good, because you don't have old loyalties. But an old feud has resurfaced, and it affects my family. I'd rather not have the head of the police department prejudiced against my family because of me."

"I won't allow an old feud to happen on my watch," Joseph said firmly.

Hazel smiled sadly and shook her head. "You won't have any choice."

Chapter Seven

The next morning, Donovan Farrington pulled his
sports car into the parking lot of the Willoughby Country
Store. Even as distracted as he was by the events going on
with the cults, he looked around the nearly empty parking
lot with surprise. He'd never seen it so deserted. He
parked close to the long, low front porch of the store and
slipped out of his car. His skin tingled as he walked past
the protective charms that had been recently added to
décor. Most customers would just assume there were
cute, rustic branch wreaths interlaced with cinnamon
sticks. But Donovan understood the use of the Rowan
branches and red thread as an ancient Celtic ward.

He lightly touched the delicate branch and, when
the electricity seared his finger, pulled back quickly.
They've upped their game, he thought, *good for them.*

Entering the store, he quickly glanced around and
found the object of his interest. Cat was in the far back
corner of the room, stocking shelves. He stared at her and

41

smiled when she stopped placing items on the display in front of her and stiffened. She slowly turned and met his eyes.

"Well met," he whispered and nodded in her direction.

Cat paused for just a moment, studying the tall, olive-skinned man that met her stare for stare. The breadth of his shoulders, the tilt of his head and the piercing, determined look in his eyes did not resemble the boy she'd fallen in love with. No, he was a man. A dangerous and strongminded man. And she had to remember that and harden her heart against any advances.

Placing the jar of calendula healing ointment back in the box, she straightened and hurried down the aisle toward Donovan. She took a deep breath to calm her nerves and appear perfectly poised, despite the butterflies fluttering in her stomach.

"What do you want?" she asked quietly, glancing around to be sure no one could overhear them.

He studied her face for a long moment and sighed. "You, Catalpa," he said roughly. "I have always wanted you."

The timbre of his voice sent a shot of desire through her system, but she wouldn't, couldn't, let him know how much he still affected her.

"We both know that's not true," she replied casually. "So, if you could move on from the ex-boyfriend act and tell me what you really came here to do, I would really appreciate it. I do have a business to run."

He cocked an eyebrow, surprised at the coolness of her tone. "Not much of a business," he retorted angrily.

Looking a little surprised at his tone, she shook her head in a disapproving manner. "Did we get up on the wrong side of the bed this morning?" she asked.

He grabbed hold of her upper arm and pulled her to the corner of the store. "Listen, we don't have time for this," he whispered harshly.

She yanked her arm out of his grasp and glared at him. "You're right, I don't have time for this," she replied. "So, say what you want to say and get out."

"They're getting bolder," he said. "They are being incited by the demon."

"You mean the Master?" she asked.

"I will not call him that," Donovan ground between his teeth. "But, yes, they are drunk on the new power he's giving them."

Cat nodded slowly. "I know," she said quietly. "Wanda went after Hazel yesterday morning in town."

Alarm and concern showed plainly on Donovan's face and Catalpa could almost believe he was sincere. "Is she okay?" he asked. "Did Wanda hurt her?"

"She's fine," Cat said, her voice softened slightly. "She handled herself well. But Wanda threatened her, threatened all of us, and it shook her up."

"What did she say?" he demanded.

"She said that she couldn't wait until the Master had us imprisoned for a very long time," Cat replied. "I

44

suppose she's not too happy that her father's in prison now."

"But that had nothing to do with you," Donovan countered.

"And she would believe that why?" Cat replied. "Of course she would assume it was us. But that doesn't matter, what matters is ending this. What matters is keeping my family safe."

"Yes, that's what matters to me too," Donovan insisted.

Cat shook her head sadly. "I could almost believe you," she said. "But then, you were always good at telling me what I wanted to hear."

"Cat, you have to…"

She lifted her hand up, to stop him. "I don't have to do anything anymore," she said. "Least of all believe you. You betrayed my trust once, I am not going to let you do it again."

"Whatever you think. Whatever you want to believe, I'm on your side," Donovan insisted. "I don't

45

want your gratitude or your trust. I just want you to know, I'm on your side."

She closed her eyes and shook her head, and when she opened her eyes and met his, her eyes were filled with regret. "Goodbye, Donovan," she said softly, then she turned and walked away.

Donovan watched her walk across the store and slip through the door marked "Employees Only." He had to regain her trust, somehow, he had to. Or his entire plan would be destroyed.

Chapter Eight

The narrow dirt road was strategically hidden behind a copse of trees and brush, and unless you knew what you were looking for, you wouldn't see it. But Joseph knew what he was looking for, because that hidden road was the pathway back to his childhood home.

He parked his vehicle far enough down the path that it would be hidden, but not close enough to offend the people of his father's village. He slipped out of the cruiser and opened the trunk, pulling out several filled shopping bags and then started the short trek to the little village at the end of the road. As he walked, he could hear the muffled sounds of traffic on the highway beyond the road. Trees and brush had been carefully cultivated along the roadway, so the entire area was hidden to the outside world.

The road slanted downwards, and Joseph took the incline easily, his long strides easily eating up the ground. He got closer to where the rough path ended near a small gap between two hills and then disappeared. He paused

before the gap and looked behind him. No one was in

sight. Quickly jogging ahead, he parted the brush, stepped

through, and immediately closed the opening behind him.

A small, Alpine village lay before him. Neat tidy

homes and shops with cream-colored plaster walls,

exposed rough timbers, open shutters with whimsical cut-

outs and window boxes filled with colorful flowers. The

road that wound through the street was cobblestone and in

the center of the square was a large pond with greenery

planted all around it. It looked like it had been lifted from

a hillside in Bavaria and planted in the middle of

Wisconsin.

As Joseph walked toward the town an uproar

began in the small schoolyard across from the square. The

children, upon seeing him, called out in glee and ran away

from their teacher, pushing open the schoolyard fence and

dashing down the street. Joseph grinned and awaited their

arrival.

"Brother Joseph!" they called. "Brother Joseph, you are back!"

"You are a bad influence on them, Brother Joseph," the middle-aged teacher called out, her face wreathed in a wide smile as she leaned against the fence to watch.

"I'm a bad influence on everybody, Sister Katrina," he called back with an answering smile. "Remember, I'm the black sheep."

She looked around in mock horror and placed her hands on her cheeks. "Don't mention sheep, you'll have the town in an uproar!"

He laughed and nodded. "I hadn't thought of that," he laughed. "Thank you for your wisdom."

She folded her arms over her chest and shook her head. "Well, at least I was able to get some teaching done today."

He chuckled. "I promise, once we are done, they will be model students for the rest of the day," he said and then he looked down at the two dozen children standing around him. "Is that not correct?"

They nodded eagerly.

"Well, then, I suppose I need to show you what I brought today," he said, squatting down in the midst of them.

Even squatting down, he was head and shoulders taller than the largest student. He reached inside the first bag and pulled out a smaller bag. "These are magic," he said softly to the students. "They are called pop rocks and you eat them."

"You eat rocks?" asked a tiny boy.

Joseph reached over and rubbed the child's head. "Not all rocks, Gustaf," he said. "Only these magic rocks." He pulled out a small packet and ripped the corner. "You pour them onto your tongue and let them stand there."

"Why?" a little girl asked.

"Well, Anna," he replied patiently. "Why don't you come here and let me show you."

With complete trust, she hurried forward, lifting her pinafore slightly to avoid the dirt on the ground, and stood next to him, her mouth wide open. He poured a small amount of the candy onto her tongue and then gently lifted her chin with his thumb, so her mouth closed. Meeting his eyes, she stared at him and waited. Suddenly her eyes widened, and she smiled with delight. "They're exploding," she cried out, then clapped her hand over her mouth and continued in a muffled voice. "They're exploding in my mouth."

"My turn!" Gustaf pleaded, stepping forward with his mouth open.

Joseph poured the rest of the small packet into the boy's mouth and he immediately closed his mouth, waiting for the results. Suddenly, he began to giggle, and a line of pink drool streamed from his mouth. Joseph grabbed his handkerchief and wiped the boy's face. "You have to keep your mouth closed, Gustaf," he teased. "Or the candy will escape."

Gustaf placed both hands over his mouth, still giggling with delight.

In a few minutes, all the children were experiencing the wonder of the exploding candy, their hands strategically in place to keep the candy inside their mouths. Joseph walked over to the teacher and handed her a large shopping bag.

"Some more things for the children," he said.

She peered into the bag and shook her head. "You must not spend all your money on the children," she said. "We have enough to meet their needs."

He placed his hand on her shoulder. "I am paid well enough that I can afford these trinkets for the children," he said. "Besides, the smiles on their faces is payment enough."

She reached in and pulled out a small white-board. "What is this?" she asked.

He pulled out a marker and opened it. Then drew on the whiteboard and wiped it off with his handkerchief. "Much better than slate boards," he said and then he

52

pulled out a set of colored markers. "And you can use colors."

She met his eyes. "And how are the village elders going to feel about this?" she asked.

He shrugged. "They probably won't like it," he said. "But I'll get my grandfather to convince them."

She chuckled softly. "And our grandfather is the only who could," she agreed.

She looked over at the children gathered together, now sticking out their newly-colored tongues at each other and laughing. "Model students," she said skeptically.

Laughing, he nodded. "Of course, they will be," he said, reaching in the bag and pulling out another bag of pop rocks. "Because you will give them more magic rocks at the end of the day."

"You and your grandfather are not that different from each other," she said wryly. "Somehow you can always get your way."

He smiled at her and nodded. "It must be in the blood," he teased.

She smiled in return. "It must be."

Chapter Nine

Joseph slowly walked up the steps to the church that sat at the far end of town. The tall steeple was the highest point in the village and the brass bell that hung within had been brought by the early settlers from their small village in Germany over 200 years ago. The ornately carved double wooden doors were worn with use and the inscription, "Wulffolk, established 1818" was barely legible.

Before he touched the door, it opened in front of him. A bear-sized man with long white hair and a flowing beard stood in the doorway. He was dressed in a long, black cassock belted in the center with a wide embroidered sash. The cassock covered a rough-woven work shirt and dark work pants. He blocked the doorway, his arms folded over his chest, his gaze piercing.

"Joseph," he said with a formal nod.

"Grandfather," Joseph replied, mirroring his grandfather's nod.

Then, suddenly, the giant man stepped forward and enfolded his grandson in a bear-like hug. He held his grandson is his arms for several long moments and then stepped back, his eyes glistening and his smile wide.

"It has been far too long," Henrich Norwalk said with a happy sigh.

"It's been two weeks," Joseph teased.

The smile widened. "Ah, but when you are dealing with a man of my advanced age, two weeks is far too long," Henrich postulated wisely. "Now what is troubling you?"

Joseph shook his head. "How do you know?"

Henrich winked. "Because, with your generation, there is always something troubling you," he said with a chuckle. Then he patted his grandson on the back and motioned him into the church. "Come, let's sit in the kitchen and we can talk."

A few minutes later, sitting across from each other at a butcher block table with meat, cheese and dark bread on a platter in front of them, Henrich nodded slowly. "So, you saw the vehicle move?"

Joseph picked up another slice a sharp cheddar cheese and bit into it before answering. "It was not that I saw the vehicle move," he explained. "It was that one moment it was in its space, and the next moment it was somewhere else."

"And did you see, on these cameras, who did the moving?"

Joseph shook his head. "No, they were out of range of the camera," he replied.

"Purposefully?" Henrich asked, cocking his head to one side.

Joseph's eyes widened, and he nodded slowly. "I had not thought of that," he said. "But, yes, I would guess that it was purposeful."

"So, there is yet some fear of reprisal in this foe," the older man said. "That is good."

"Why? Why is it good?" Joseph asked. "I feel you have more information about this matter than I do."

Henrich sat back in his large wooden chair, the wood groaning at his weight, and folded his arms across his ample chest. "There have been signs that a reckoning is coming."

"A reckoning?" he asked. "Yesterday, Hazel Willoughby, the owner of the pickup that was moved, said there was an old feud awakening."

Henrich's eyes widened. "A Willoughby, you say," he replied softly. "A Willoughby was targeted. That is very interesting."

"You know of the Willoughbys?" Joseph asked. "Why?"

"They are of an old family, just like ours," he said. "They have abilities that have made some fear them, and others seek them out. They have not been our enemies over the years."

"Have they been our friends?"

Henrich sighed sadly. "We have no friends, Joseph," he said. "We cannot risk having friends. But those who are not our enemies, we hold in great respect."

58

"Do you trust them?" Joseph asked.

"A Willoughby saved your father's life when he was a boy," Henrich said, meeting his grandson's eyes. "She nearly lost her own life to do it, but she was willing to sacrifice herself for a strange child. That tells me much about the Willoughbys. I would trust them with my life."

"But not with our secret," Joseph countered.

Henrich shook his head. "No. No, I trust no one with our secret."

Chapter Ten

Hazel walked into the kitchen and headed straight for the refrigerator.

"Wash your hands before you eat anything," her mother called from the counter.

"I'm just grabbing a bottle of water," Hazel replied, pulling a bottle from the refrigerator door.

Agnes put down the chopping knife and walked across the kitchen, her hand extended. "At least let me open it for you, so you don't get germs into it," she insisted.

Laughing, Hazel handed her mom the plastic bottle. "You know, I could have opened it myself, without using my hands," she teased.

Agnes sighed. "Yes, I know," she admitted. "But sometimes a mom likes to be useful."

"You are always useful," Hazel said. "Even when we pretend you're not."

Opening the bottle, Agnes handed it back to Hazel and then studied her daughter for a moment. "Are you ready to talk about it?" she asked.

Hazel took a long drink of the cold water and then looked back at her mom. "Talk about what?" she asked, feigning ignorance.

"Fine, I can wait," Agnes said, turning and returning to the counter where the vegetables for a stir-fry were being chopped.

Hazel followed her mother and sat on the bar stool on the other side of the counter. Her mother handed her an apron. "If you're going to sit there, you need to cover your work clothes up," she insisted.

"Oh, for goodness sakes," Hazel said, and then with a wave of her hand, she was completely changed into clean clothes and her hair was pulled back in a ponytail. "Better?"

Her mother bit back a grin. "Much better," she replied, as she chopped zucchini. "So, what aren't we talking about?"

Hazel smiled. "We aren't talking about the new Chief of Police and how I nearly melted when he touched my hand yesterday."

"He touched your hand?" Agnes asked.

"Well, after Fuzzy attacked him…"

The knife clattered to the countertop. "Fuzzy attacked the chief of police?" Agnes cried, aghast. "What happened? Was he hurt? Why would Fuzzy do such a thing?"

Hazel grabbed a piece of zucchini and bit into it. "I have no idea," she replied calmly. "Joseph thought that Fuzzy might have been protecting me." She shrugged easily. "But he handled it. Once Fuzzy knocked him over and was on top of him, he kind of grabbed Fuzzy's face and started to talk to him. Suddenly, they're like old friends."

"I'm really going to have to have a talk with Fuzzy about this," Agnes said, picking up her knife and chopping loudly. "I mean, really, the chief of police!"

"Yeah, so my knees are a little weak after I witness this whole thing," Hazel continued. "And so, he gets up first and offers me a hand up. As soon as I touch his hand – blingo."

"Blingo?" Agnes asked.

"Blingo," Hazel repeated. "My body gets all warm and tingly and hot and bothered and on edge and relaxed, all at the same time."

"I always wondered what blingo meant," Agnes said wryly.

"Mother, this is serious," Hazel said with an impatient huff. "I mean, I've never felt anything like this. It was life-changing."

"For him too?" Agnes asked.

Hazel sighed. "I could tell he was feeling something too," she said. "But I guess he didn't want his life to be changed, because he backed off like I was scorching him."

"Really?" Agnes asked. "Well, that's odd."

"Right?" Hazel agreed, snatching another piece of zucchini. "So, I went inside and got the ticket for him."

"What ticket?"

"The ticket he gave me for parking in front of a fire hydrant," she replied. "He said he'd made a mistake and I was innocent."

"Why would he say that?" Agnes asked.

Hazel puzzled over that question for a moment. "Well, I guess he could have watched the video camera footage from Harley's place," she said. "And seen that I originally parked behind the store."

"Wouldn't you think that if he'd seen the footage, he would be asking a bunch of questions?" Agnes asked. "I know I would have."

"Would have what?" Cat asked, coming into through the back door.

"The new police chief came over yesterday afternoon and took back the ticket he gave Hazel for parking in front of a fire hydrant," Agnes replied. "He said he'd made a mistake."

Cat looked over at Hazel. "What do you think?"

"I think he must have seen the footage and saw the truck was moved by someone else," she said. "He seemed regretful, well, at first."

"Then how did he seem?" Cat asked.

Hazel turned in her seat and looked at her sister. "Why? What happened?" she asked.

"Donovan stopped by this morning," Cat admitted. "He said that we needed to be careful. He said the others were becoming bolder and more powerful."

"Well, that's just what I wanted to hear," Agnes said. "We need to open Henry's grimoire and read what's next."

Cat closed her eyes and stood still for a moment, then opened her eyes and shook her head. "I don't feel that it's time yet," she said. "Something else has to happen."

"What?" Hazel asked.

Cat shook her head. "I don't know," she said. "But there's still a link missing."

"Well, we need to hurry up and find your missing link," Hazel said. "Because the other side is raring to go."

Chapter Eleven

"I'd like to see her," Joseph said to his grandfather after they'd finished their lunch.

Henrich closed his eyes slowly and shook his head. "It will do you no good," he said. "There has been no change."

Joseph lifted up a shopping bag and placed it on the table. "I brought these," he said. "They are new, experimental drugs. They could help her."

"How did you get those?" Henrich asked.

"I have ways," Joseph replied. "You don't have to worry about it."

Henrich reached over and grabbed his grandson's arm. "You speak too lightly," he said. "You say I don't have to worry, but of course I do. If you are caught and imprisoned, how long will it take others to discover our secret? How long until there are people searching for us? How long until our lives are destroyed?"

"You can't let fear rule us," Joseph argued. "It has ruled us long enough. It is killing little Gabriella. It has killed others. When do we stand up and let people know who we are?"

"Never!" Henrich whispered harshly. "Never do we tell. Never do we show. We learned our lesson two hundred years ago. Why do you think we came here and made our home among the hills?"

"You mean made your hiding place among the hills," Joseph said. "This is not a home, it's a cage. We dare not go out. Dare not be seen. What kind of life is that?"

"It is the kind of life that has kept us safe for two hundred years," Henrich replied, patting his grandson on his arm. "It is the kind of life that most of us choose."

"Not my father," Joseph said.

Henrich nodded and smiled sadly. "And you see what it got him."

"Happiness," Joseph replied quickly, his voice hoarse with emotion. "Even for a short time, it brought him happiness."

Joseph stood up and lifted the final bag. "I have a gift for her," he said. "I will not take much of her time or overtax her strength."

Henrich stood and placed an arm around Joseph's neck and pulled him close for another hug. "You take the time you need," he said softly. "And we will try the medicines. But please, please be careful. Not for me. Not for our village. But for yourself."

"I will, grandfather," Joseph whispered. "I promise, I will."

He turned and walked away from the old man, his shoes echoing against the old wood floor. He opened the kitchen door, closed it behind him, and then walked over to the narrow staircase leading up to the personal apartments above the church. He climbed the stairs and walked down the dark hallway. At the end of the hall, he tapped lightly on the door and then pushed the door open.

69

"Hello, Gabriella," he said as he peeked around the doorway.

"Joseph!" the tiny girl squealed with delight, but then was hit by a spasm of coughing.

Joseph hurried to her side and lifted the glass of liquid sitting on her nightstand. "Here," he said gently, lifting the glass to her lips. "Just sip. It will ease the cough."

The girl obediently sipped and the coughing subsided.

"How does it taste?" he asked.

She screwed up her face. "Like old leather and fish oil," she replied.

"I think I would rather cough," he teased.

She grinned up at him. "I agree with you," she said. "Too bad Sister Helga does not agree with us."

This time Joseph screwed up his face. "Sister Helga?" he asked. "Does she make you take that other awful potion she creates?"

The grin spread to a wide smile. "Yes!" Gabriella said with an eager nod. "She makes me take it every single day."

Joseph reached into the bag and pulled out a stuffed teddy bear. "Well, I brought you this to keep you company," he said. "And to reward you for taking all the medicine Sister Helga gives you."

He placed the bear in the child's arms and watched her draw it close and cuddle it. "It's so soft," Gabriella purred. "I have never felt anything so soft."

"It's a magical bear," Joseph said to her, sitting on the side her bed and pushing her bangs away from her forehead. "You can talk to it and tell it all of your secrets."

"Will it make me better?" she asked hopefully.

He felt his throat tighten with emotion, and he nodded slowly. "Well, I suppose we shall see, won't we?" he asked.

"Then we can run together," she said, her eyes gleaming with hope. "We shall run for miles and miles."

He leaned forward and pressed a kiss on her forehead. "Yes, we will," he agreed. "And no one will be able to catch us."

She leaned back on her pillow, still clutching the bear, her face wan and her breathing shallow. "I'm a little bit tired, Uncle Joseph," she whispered.

He pulled the blankets up to her chin and tucked her in. "Well, you and your new friend should take a nap," he whispered. "Pleasant dreams, sweet one."

She yawned and nodded. "Thank you, Joseph," she said quietly, then closed her eyes and fell asleep.

Joseph slowly stood up, careful not to jar the bed and the sleeping child, and back out of the room, closing the door softly behind him.

"I hope you didn't mean what you said about my medicines," a woman's voice said behind him.

He turned quickly, nearly hitting his head against the low, sloped ceiling, and saw a young, raven-haired woman dressed in a red and black dirndl standing before him. Her long, dark hair was held back by a red scarf that matched her apron, and the black and red embroidered dirndl underneath the apron was decorated with fine needlepoint hearts and flowers. Her black corset was laced tightly across her small waist, further emphasizing her décolletage that displayed in an off-the-shoulder peasant blouse. She looked up at Joseph with a little pout on her red lips.

"Helga," he replied, surprised and a little ashamed of his comments. "No. No, of course not," he stammered. "We were just having a little bit of fun."

"Fun, at my expense?" she asked.

He shook his head. "No, fun in order to make a very sick child laugh," he said sternly, not allowing himself to be pulled into her game.

She moved closer to him and placed her hand on his arm. "Please forgive me, Joseph," she said. She lifted wide-eyes to him that seemed to be filled with sorrow. "It's just that I know I have done everything I can, but little Gabriella is not getting better."

He patted her hand gently. "We all know how tirelessly you have worked to keep her well," he said.

"But I will be the one to bear the blame if she does not recover," she said.

"We did not blame you when Peter did not recover," he replied, wondering how this conversation went from Gabriella's needs to Helga's. "I think we all realize that in order to continue our security, we are limited in our choices."

She stepped up even closer to him. "Do you believe that, Joseph?" she asked, her voice a breathy whisper.

"Of course I do," he said. "I would not have offered those words if I did not believe them."

"You are so good with the children," she continued, sliding her other hand onto his other arm. "I do not think the others realize how much time you spend visiting the sick children. And you, a man without a family of your own."

Joseph tried to step back to create a little distance between he and Helga, but the slope of the roof caught him in place. "I'm concerned about the children," he said. "They are part of our community. They are our future."

"And your future, Joseph," she asked, sliding her hands further up his arms. "What do you want for your future? A willing wife? Strong children of your own?"

Suddenly they both heard coughing from inside the bedroom. Joseph started to turn, but she held him in place. "She will be fine," she insisted. "She just needs to get it out of her system."

Surprised at her vehemence, Joseph pushed her hands off his arms. "That may be true," he said. "But I cannot bear to hear her cough like that without going to her. Excuse me."

Chapter Twelve

Donovan parked his car in the underground parking garage beneath his building. He stepped out, clicked his fob to lock the car and turned to head to the staircase.

"Hello, Donovan," the woman's voice came from directly behind him.

He stopped but didn't turn around. "I'm in a hurry, Wanda," he said curtly.

He felt her hand slide over his shoulder, smelled her musky perfume and heard her breath in his ear. "I can do hurry," she whispered.

He felt her press her body against his back and realized that her obvious attempt to seduce him had absolutely no effect on him. "That would cheapen us both," he replied.

He heard the sharp hiss and then his body was swung around to face her. He saw the rage in her face and caught her arm before she moved it again, possibly

76

sending him across the lot and into the concrete walls. "No. You don't get to take your tantrum out on me," he said deliberately.

She struggled to pull her arm out of his grasp, but he held it securely.

"You're nothing," she finally spat at him. "You were a guttersnipe, an outcast, no one wanted you. You think those Willoughbys are great, the Master told me that they just used you. They needed your power, they needed your skills. They were just amassing an army and you were an easy recruit."

Donovan didn't allow the words, thoughts he'd often wondered himself, change his demeanor. He merely stared down at her and curled his lip in disdain. "The Master and I have already had conversations about the Willoughbys and their influence in my life," he said firmly. "And he knows that I am loyal to the cause."

"Does he know you were kissing up to Cat this morning?" she asked with a satisfied smile.

"He sent me," Donovan replied easily. "But I'm sure he didn't tell you, probably because he knows he really can't trust you to keep your mouth shut."

Her eyes widened for a moment and then narrowed them, studying Donovan carefully. "So, you're the one who decided on the strike this evening?"

Donovan's heart lurched, but he allowed his mouth to curve into a slight smile. "Who else would the Master choose to select a target?" he asked.

"I almost don't believe you," she replied, slowly shaking her head. "I almost don't think you know about the attack on the Willoughbys tonight."

His heart pounding in his chest, he met her eyes directly. "You can believe what you want to believe," he said. "As a matter of fact, the Master would prefer it if people were confused about which side of the war I'm on."

"Like a double agent," she said softly, nodding her head with delight. "So, those bitches think you're with them and they're going to trust you with their secrets."

"The Master has asked me not to confirm or deny those kinds of questions," he replied, releasing her hand. "And I won't, as long as we understand each other."

She stepped back and nodded. "I want to be there when they find out that their beloved Donovan betrayed them," she laughed. "I want to see the look on their faces, especially Cat's face, when she discovers you were part of the group that destroyed their store. Those Willoughbys have had it coming for a long time."

Donovan hardened his gaze and thinned his lips. "And it's comments like yours that are going to destroy our side," he said harshly. "How do you know that I'm not a traitor? How do you know that I'm not going to tell the Willoughby's about the attack on their store? You need to be a lot more discreet, or you will be more of a hindrance to the cause than a help."

Wanda shrugged and smiled. "Even if you were a traitor, there's nothing you can do about it now," she said. "The explosives have already been planted and set. The party's going to start in fifteen minutes. There's absolutely nothing you could do." She shook her head and smiled. "But you knew that. You're just trying to confuse me."

"You passed the test, Wanda," he said with an approving smile. "Now, I have to get to my office and you need to get somewhere public, so we both have alibis."

"Oh, right," she said, nodding. "I'm supposed to be at Harley's. Everyone knows that Harley is a friend to the Willoughby's, so he wouldn't lie for the coven. It's the perfect place."

She turned and hurried across the parking garage, her footsteps echoing as she went.

Donovan turned and ran to the steps, taking them by threes, he dashed down the corridor and into his office. He started to call Cat, but then stopped. "They'll know," he whispered. "They'll know I called her."

His finally pressed 9-1-1 and waited for dispatch to answer.

"9-1-1, what's your emergency?"

"There's a fire at the Willoughby Store out on Highway P. Please send the fire department and an ambulance," he said, praying that there would be no need to it. "Please hurry!"

"Can I get your…" the operator was cut off when Donovan hung up his phone.

He glanced at the clock, it was 4:45, the time Cat was locking things up and putting away the cash drawer. He closed his eyes and pictured her in his mind. "Cat, get out of there," he called, trying to send his message telepathically. "Cat, seek shelter. Cat, hide! Now!"

Chapter Thirteen

Once he'd been able to calm Gabriella's coughing spasm, Joseph had slipped out of the room, avoiding Helga, and said his goodbyes to his grandfather before jogging back to his vehicle. With his vehicle stopped at the end of the road, he rolled down the window and listened for any traffic on the highway before him. Hearing none, he crept forward, around the copse of trees and then onto the grass-covered drive that was barely discernable to the shoulder of the road. No one was around, so he quickly pulled onto the highway and headed back to Whitewater.

He was two miles east of the junction of County Roads A and P when he heard the call about a fire at the Willoughby Store come over the radio. His heart dropped and he immediately pictured Hazel in the midst of fire and flames. Pulling over to the side of the road, he picked up the discarded ticket and punched in the phone number listed next to her name.

"Hello?" her voice seemed clear and slightly confused.

Joseph pulled back out of the road as he replied. "Are you okay?"

"I'm fine," she replied. "Why?"

"The fire, at your store," he said. "Is everything okay?"

"There is no fire at the…"

Joseph could hear the explosion in the background. "Hazel!" he yelled into the phone. "Hazel, answer me!"

The phone went dead. Joseph turned on his sirens and accelerated, driving past farm houses and fields at full-speed. He could hear the fire trucks in the distance and wondered who reported the fire before it already began. Obviously, someone involved in setting the fire.

He switched on the radio and called dispatch.

"This is Chief Norwalk, who called in the 911 on the Willoughby fire?" he asked.

"I'll have to check on that," the dispatcher replied. "Can I call you back?"

"Yeah," he said. "Call me as soon as you know."

He could see plumes of smoke in the distance when he turned up Highway P and swore under his breath. The flames were already visible above the tree line. He hoped there would be something left of the store by the time the fire department arrived.

Chapter Fourteen

Hazel dropped her phone when she heard the blast and immediately turned toward the store, concentrating her inner vision on her sister, Cat. ""Bacainn!" she cried out, creating a barrier between her sister and any projectiles caused by the explosion. Then she took off running toward the store.

The rest of the family poured out the house, running towards the store. Agnes felt a little relief when she saw there were no cars in the parking lot, but that relief was short-lived when she saw the flames burst through the roof of the store.

Hazel rushed past them, only glancing over her shoulder for a moment. "Where's Henry?" she yelled.

"He went to town," Rowan shouted back, trying to catch up with her sister.

"Call him and have him come home," Hazel replied. "We might need both of you!"

Then she darted ahead and ran to the front door, ripping it open with a wave of her hand.

"Cat!" she screamed at the top of her lungs.

"In here," Cat cried out. "I'm in the office and thanks to your damn spell, I can't move."

Hazel inhaled a shuddering breath and then moved forward, pushing the debris and fire to the side as she hurried to the back of the store. "Sorry," she called out, once she could speak. "That was the first thing that came to mind."

She opened the door with another wave of her hand, and found her sister crouched beneath the metal desk. "How did you know?" she asked, removing the spell and allowing her sister to climb out of her hiding place.

"I heard someone calling for me to seek shelter," she said. "I wasn't sure what was supposed to happen, so I locked the front door, ran back to the office and hid under my desk."

"Well, whoever called you, I'm grateful," Hazel said, stepping back and letting Cat see what was left of her store. "They probably saved your life."

"Cat! Hazel!" Agnes called from the front door. "Are you okay?"

"We're fine, Mom," Hazel called back. "Just assessing the damage."

Then Hazel turned back to Cat. "So, we have a choice here," she said.

"Okay," Cat said, her stomach sinking as she looked around. "Give me my options."

"We let the fire department arrive and hack the hell out of the rest of the store, and then have them do an investigation on who caused this mess," Hazel began.

"And option two?" Cat asked.

"I clean things up, tell them it was a false alarm, and we find out who did this ourselves."

Cat looked around the room again. "It's going to take a lot out of you to fix this," she said.

Hazel shrugged. "So, I'll get some bath salts, herb tea, and do a facial in the bath tonight," she said. "I'll get over it."

Cat put her arms around her sister and gave her a hug. "Thank you," she said.

"Well, thanks for not being dead," Hazel replied, her voice cracking. "You scared the hell out of me."

"If it's any comfort, I scared the hell out of me too," Cat said.

Hazel nodded. "Okay, it's a little comfort, but not much," she said with a tight smile. "Now, let's get this cleaned up before the fire trucks arrive."

Chapter Fifteen

Joseph was two miles away from the Willoughby Store when he noticed a strange cloud appear in the sky. It was dark and thick and rolled forward, enveloping the tops of the trees and blocking any smoke or flames.

"What the..." he exclaimed, staring at the clouds that moved in a circular motion around the area.

He wondered if it could be the remnants of a chemical explosion. He knew the Willoughbys also created herbal mixtures in another building on the farm. Could that building have been affected by the explosion? Did they have an LP tank outside the store? Could that have exploded too?

Once again, the vision of Hazel's body, torn and bleeding, entered his mind. He saw her laying in the rubble of the store, burnt and broken. He could feel rage surge through his system, whoever did this to her would pay. Whether through the laws of the land, or the laws of the Wulffolk, they would pay. But now, his only goal was to make sure she was safe.

His squad car careened into the parking lot at the store, its sirens blasting and its tire throwing out a spray of gravel. He pulled in front of the store and stared in total disbelief. Everything was fine. The store looked no different than it had earlier in the day when he had passed it on the road. He got out of his vehicle and looked around. There was no smell of smoke, the sky above him was bright blue, and the strange cloud was now gone.

He started to walk toward the store when the door opened, and he saw Hazel, her eyes closed, leaning on two women in order to walk. Acting on sheer impulse, he ran forward and scooped her up in his arms. "What did you do to her?" he demanded.

"Listen to me," the tall red-head said to him, her eyes filled with wrath. "You put my sister down and you put her down slowly, or you'll be sorry."

The tall, black-haired woman stepped forward and put her hand on the red-head. "You need to listen to my

90

sister," she said, and although her voice was calm, he could sense the steel underneath it. "You have no idea what we are capable of."

Hazel opened her eyes and looked up at Joseph. "What are you doing here?" she mumbled.

"You know him?" Rowan asked.

Hazel sighed softly and nodded. "Police Chief Norwalk meet my sisters, Rowan and Catalpa," she said.

He looked down at her, his panic beginning to subside. "What happened?" he asked. "I saw the flames. I saw the fire."

Agnes came out of the building, closing the door behind her and then turned. "Hazel you did an excellent job..." she began and then stopped when she saw Joseph. "Who are you and why are holding my daughter?"

Joseph shook his head. "I'm Chief Norwalk," he said.

"Oh, the nice young man who took back Hazel's ticket," Agnes said, moving forward and smiling at him. "I do apologize for Fuzzy's behavior. It's not at all like him to attack someone."

Confused at the turn of events, Joseph felt like he had stepped into an alternative universe. "Can someone please answer my questions?" he asked.

The fire truck sirens suddenly seemed much closer. Agnes turned in their direction. "It seems to me that it took those fire trucks quite a long time to get to our store," she said to no one in particular. Then she looked at Joseph. "Wouldn't you agree?"

He thought about it for a moment. He received the call when he was easily ten miles away from the store. The fire trucks were several miles closer and he had been there for several minutes. He nodded at her. "Yes, I would agree," he said.

She smiled at him. "Well, perhaps you wouldn't mind carrying Hazel inside," she said. "While we greet the firefighters."

"But…" he began.

"You might as well do what she's says," Hazel said, yawning softly. "She always gets her own way."

"Is that so?" he asked, his voice gentle as her eyes drifted shut and snuggled against him.

"Um, hmmm," she sighed sleepily.

"I guess I'd better listen then," he whispered. He hefted her a little closer. "Where to?" he asked Agnes, as Rowan and Cat walked across the parking lot towards the road.

"Why don't you take this back path," Agnes suggested. "Then you are both out of the view of prying eyes."

Joseph walked down the path and was around the back corner of the house when the fire trucks pulled up in front of the house. Fuzzy stood on the deck, his tail wagging, eagerly greeting both of them.

"You don't seem too worried about her," Joseph said to the wolf.

The wolf whined softly and then led Joseph into the house. Joseph stepped into the kitchen and

93

immediately saw that it was left in a hurry. A pot on the stove had charred stir-fry cooking in it, the water was still running in the sink and an empty meat container was laying on the floor. He looked over at Fuzzy and then looked back at the meat container. "Taking advantage of the situation?" he asked.

The wolf had the courtesy to at least look a little ashamed.

"Okay, show me where to safely lay her down," he said and then followed the dog to a comfortable couch in the middle of the great room. He laid her down, tucked a comforter around her and then went back into the kitchen, pushing the wok off the burner, turning off the water and then squatting down and disposing of the meat container in the garbage.

"You owe me," he said to the wolf, who licked his cheek in gratitude.

"Fuzzy usually doesn't take to strangers," Rowan said, as she walked into the kitchen. "But strangers usually don't help him hide his nefarious deeds."

Fuzzy sat down and looked up at Rowan, his mouth open in a wide wolf smile. Joseph stood up, dwarfing Rowan, which was something that rarely happened to her.

"Are you going to tell me what's going on?" he asked.

She shook her head. "Oh, no," she replied with a smile. "You are going to have to get the story from the whole family. And that's an experience not to be missed."

Chapter Sixteen

Henry stormed through the front door. "I just passed a bunch of fire trucks on their way back to town. What the hell happened here?" he exclaimed immediately.

Joseph, sitting in a chair next to the couch, looked up at Henry. "That's what I'm trying to discover too," he said, unfolding his tall body from the chair. "But so far everyone is telling me that I have to wait until Henry gets back. I take it you're Henry."

Henry closed the door and walked over to Joseph. "I am," he said guardedly. "And you are?"

"Chief Joseph Norwalk," Joseph replied easily. "The new police chief in Whitewater."

Henry stood his ground, assessing the man before him. "And have you been bought and paid for?"

"That's an interesting question," Joseph said, nodding slowly. "And generally, I would have taken offense if anyone else had asked me it. But after what I've seen today, I can understand your concern."

Henry folded his arms over his chest. "Well, have you?" he asked pointedly.

Joseph smiled and shook his head. "No, the only pay I receive is my salary from the city," he replied, meeting Henry's eyes. "And the only side I take is the one that's on the right side of the law."

"Good," Henry replied.

"But I've yet to determine which side of the law you're on," Joseph added pointedly.

"That's fair enough," Henry said. "Do you have an open mind?"

"How open?" Joseph asked.

This time Henry smiled. "Very open," he said.

"I guess we're all going to find out," Agnes said, as she entered the room carrying a tray of teacups. "I thought we could use some tea to calm our nerves."

"Why do our nerves have to be calmed?" Henry asked.

Rowan hurried into the room, followed by Cat.

"I'll explain in a moment," Rowan said. "But can you first help me with Hazel?"

"Hazel?" Henry asked, then he turned and saw her on the couch. "What happened? Why is she…"

"She's just exhausted," Rowan interrupted, calming him. "And normally I would suggest we just let her sleep. But since she's an integral part of this conversation, I thought if we both worked on her…"

"We could share the burden," Henry finished. "That's brilliant."

"Burden?" Joseph asked, as he watched Rowan and Henry kneel on the floor next to the couch. "What are you talking about?"

"Shhh," Agnes said. "They really need to concentrate."

Rowan placed her hands on Hazel's shoulders and Henry laid his hands over Rowan's. They both closed their eyes and Rowan spoke first,

The cost of magic is high indeed,

It pulls the strength right out of thee,

Then Henry spoke,

In lieu we offer our energy,

As we ask, so mote it be.

Fascinated, Joseph watched as Rowan and Henry both seemed to experience physical signs of exhaustion; their breathing increased, sweat beaded on their foreheads and their bodies shook slightly. Then, when they lifted their hands and sat back on heels, Hazel sat up on the couch looking totally refreshed.

"I could have just slept it off," she said to Henry and Rowan. "You didn't need to put yourselves at risk."

"We did it together," Rowan said. "So, the risk was minimized."

"Would someone mind telling me what is going on here?" Joseph asked.

Shocked to hear his voice, Hazel turned and looked across the room at him. "What are you doing here?" she asked.

"You might not remember, dear," Agnes said. "But Joseph arrived just as Rowan and Cat were carrying you out of the store. He carried you inside."

Hazel paused to remember and then a flush rose on her cheeks as she recalled snuggling against his chest. She took a deep breath and nodded. "Yes, now that you mention it, I seem to remember the chief arriving on the scene." She met Joseph's eyes. "Thank you for helping me."

"I don't want your thanks," he said. "I want an explanation."

"Well, family, what do you think?" Agnes asked.

"He's going to hear about it one way or the other," Rowan said. "It would probably be better for him to hear the truth from us."

"Cat?" Agnes asked.

Cat turned and studied Joseph until he felt that she was looking inside of him.

"Yes," she said slowly. "Yes, he needs to know from us."

100

"Henry?" Agnes asked.

Henry smiled at Agnes, aware of the honor she just placed on him, considering him to be part of their family. "Thank you," he said. "I like the man. I think he's direct and honest. And whether he likes it or not, he's going to be part of this."

Agnes nodded. "I agree," she said. "Henry, why don't you begin by telling Joseph about the history of the Willoughbys in Whitewater."

Henry sat down, the couch at his back and looked at Joseph. "There were three sisters who traveled from New England, Salem to be precise, to escape what they feared would be a new resurgence of witch trials. They initially came to Whitewater, Wisconsin, which seemed to be a Midwestern Mecca for many coming from New England. They settled well, contributed to the community, and were well respected."

"Very well respected," Agnes added. "And everything would have been fine, if it hadn't been for Morris Pratt."

Henry nodded. "Morris Pratt was a gentleman who was interested in spiritualism, which was thriving in the United States during that same time period. He was looking for a place to build a school to teach spiritualism and do academic research. He built a large institute in Whitewater because the area was already active in a paranormal way."

Joseph nodded. "I've heard that about this area," he said. "So, what happened?"

"What I used to think was legend, and now understand as fact, is that the people at the institute were playing with fire. They were having seances and opening themselves up to any kind of entity that would answer. Because of their ignorance, they unleashed something—a demon, an ancient evil entity, or a spirit bent on mayhem."

"Unleashed it?" Joseph asked.

"Opened a portal from wherever it had been into our world," Hazel said. "Where it could destroy the people of Whitewater and then move on from there."

"It had to be defeated," Henry continued. "But the only way to defeat it was for three sisters, The Willoughby sisters, to work together and cast a spell on the creature that would bind it for one hundred and twenty years. They knew in order for the spell to work, there would have to be a sacrifice. In this case, the sacrifice was their lives."

"Before the sisters placed the spell on the demon, they had their family move away from the city," Agnes said. "Not only to escape the repercussions if something went wrong with the spell, but also to escape the hard feelings from the other coven in the area."

"There were two covens in Whitewater?" Joseph asked.

"Well, it used to be one," Cat replied. "Until many of the members thought they could control the demon and use its power to influence the world around them."

"What happened to the other coven?" Joseph asked.

"It's alive and well in Whitewater," Hazel said. "Alive and well and busy moving pickup trucks."

103

"So, this feud has been going on for a hundred years?" he asked.

Hazel shook her head. "No, actually, we've lived side-by-side for a long time with no problems," she replied. "Well, little problems, but nothing we couldn't handle. The stakes have been upped recently."

"What do you mean by that? Upped?" Joseph asked.

"One of the members shot Henry," Rowan said. "Because they found out he was a part of this."

"Shot?" Joseph repeated, incredulous.

"In the chest," Hazel added. "It wasn't a warning shot."

"Did you call the police?" Joseph asked.

"Did you know that the former police chief was actually the uncle of the man who shot Henry?" Rowan asked. "And when he came to the hospital, he told us he had witnesses that saw Henry shoot himself."

Joseph looked at Henry. "It's pretty damn hard to shoot yourself in the chest," he said sarcastically.

"Tell me about it," Henry replied.

"I do know that the old police chief ended up in prison," he said. "But it was for drugs, not..."

"Being a member of a coven who wants to unleash a demon?" Hazel inserted.

Nodding, Joseph smiled. "I could see how that would be a hard offense to prosecute." Then he began to feel a pit in his stomach, as if he knew the answer but was loath to ask the question. "But, why all of a sudden? If things were quiet, why are they bringing this up now?"

"The one hundred and twenty years are over," Agnes said. "And my daughters are the chosen ones destined to fight the demon."

Fear increased the pit in his stomach, he looked across the room and met Hazel's eyes. "Tell me it's a lie," he pleaded.

Her eyes filled with sadness and she barely shook her head, but he knew that everything they'd told him was the truth.

Chapter Seventeen

"So, tell me about the explosion," Joseph insisted. "And don't leave anything out."

"Explosion?" Henry exclaimed, looking around the room at all of the Willoughbys. "Explosion?"

"The store exploded," Cat said, trying for a casual shrug, but still quaking on the inside. "But Hazel was able to protect me and undo the damage."

"We're fine," Rowan said, placing her hand on Henry's arm. "Really. We're all fine."

"Fine? You're all fine?" Henry raged. "Cat was nearly killed. Your store blown up. And just because no one died you think you're fine?" He turned to Joseph. "This is attempted murder, isn't it?"

"Well, it depends on if it happened or not," he said slowly. "So, let's start from the beginning."

"Okay, that would be me," Hazel said. "You called me and asked me about the fire."

Joseph nodded. "I heard over dispatch that there was a fire at the Willoughby store, so I called you."

"And then the store exploded," Hazel said.

"Wait," Henry interrupted. "Someone called the fire in before it happened?"

"Yeah, that's more than a little suspicious," Joseph said to Henry. "Which is why I called dispatch to have them check on the caller i.d. on that call." He turned to back to Hazel. "Okay, so the last thing I knew was I heard an explosion and then you must have dropped your phone."

She winced and nodded. "Sorry, I didn't even think of that," she said. "I heard the explosion and immediately put a shield around Cat to protect her."

"Put a shield?" Joseph asked.

Henry sent Joseph a sympathetic smile. "Been there, felt that," he said. "Let me give you a little advice here, you need to suspend disbelief and open yourself up to possibilities that you'd never imagined."

"Thank you," Joseph replied, with a thoughtful nod. "I'll see what I can do." He turned back to Hazel. "A shield?"

She shrugged. "A picture is worth a thousand words," she muttered and then she waved her arm in his direction. "Bacainn!"

As soon as the word was out of her mouth, she picked up a pillow and whipped it in his direction. Joseph ducked, but then stared wide-eyed when the pillow stopped six-inches from his face and slid to the ground. "Do that again," he insisted.

Smiling, she threw another pillow at him and once again, it hit an invisible barrier and slid down.

"That's amazing," he said.

Secretly waving her arm and dispelling the shield, she grinned at Joseph, "How about one more for good luck?" she asked sweetly.

Joseph shrugged. "Lay it on me," he encouraged.

Like a fabric football, Hazel hiked a bolster pillow over her shoulder at Joseph. Smiling confidently, he watched it sail through the air towards him and finally, at the last moment, his eyes widened in surprise when he realized it wasn't going to stop. The pillow caught him right in the middle of his face and knocked him backwards in the chair.

"Hey!" he exclaimed, pushing the pillow off his lap.

Hazel's grin widened. "Oh, sorry, I guess I forgot to tell you that I ended the spell," she said, biting back the laughter.

"I guess you did," he replied, then, quick as a wink, he threw the pillow back at her.

She caught it before it hit her and laughed delightedly. "How did I know you were going to do that?" she asked.

"Because you would have done the exact same thing?" he asked.

She nodded. "Exactly," she said and then her smiled lessened. "So, do you believe that we are unique?"

He met her eyes. "I knew you were unique the moment I saw you," he said softly, and Hazel felt a thrill shoot through her. Then he turned to the rest of the family. "But, yes, I believe you and the rest of your family have special powers that go beyond usual capabilities."

Hazel took a deep breath and then continued, "Once I sent the shield, I started to run towards the store," she said. "I pass Mom and Rowan who are running from the house. I tell Rowan to call Henry and get him back home."

"Why?" Joseph asked.

Hazel shook her head. "What?"

"Why did you want Rowan to call Henry?" he asked.

"Because I didn't know what I was going to find once I entered the store," she explained. "And they're both healers. In case..." She paused, glanced over at Cat and her eyes filled with tears. "In case..."

She stopped, closed her eyes, and shook her head. "I can't," she whispered, her voice cracking as she placed her hand over her mouth.

Cat walked over to her sister, sat down next to her and hugged her. "What she's trying to say is that she didn't know if her shield was fast enough," Cat explained. "But it was. It was perfect."

Hazel looked up at her sister, tears streaming down her face. "I was so afraid," she admitted. "So afraid that I was too late. And I would have been if you hadn't been under your desk."

"Why were you under your desk?" Agnes asked.

"I heard a voice telling me to run and hide," she replied.

"Whose voice?" Joseph asked.

Cat took a deep breath. "I think it was Donovan," she replied. "I nearly didn't do it because of spite, but I could sense the urgency and it frightened me."

"Donovan?" Joseph asked.

"Donovan Farrington," Cat said.

Joseph cocked his head to the side and nodded slowly. "Well, isn't that interesting," he said. "Because Donovan Farrington was the name of the person who called 9-1-1 about the fire."

Chapter Eighteen

Donovan stared at the name etched into the gold plate on the heavy oak door with a feeling of trepidation. Mayor Edgar Bates. He'd received a succinct text "Come to my office now," from the mayor only a few minutes ago and, although it went against every fiber of his being to respond to an order, he knew he had no choice. City Hall was deserted, as it was well after business hours, so he knew that he and the mayor were the only witnesses to the clandestine meeting.

He lifted his hand and rapped on the oak door.

"Enter," came the terse reply from inside.

Donovan opened the door and looked over at the mayor sitting behind his large desk. Edgar Bates, a stout man with graying temples, slowly looked up and met Donovan's eyes. There was little in the mayor's appearance to intimidate, he was about five feet ten inches, much shorter than Donovan. His portly physique might have at one time been muscular, but now it was flaccid and soft. His hairline had receded to the back of his head and his eyes were hidden behind a thick pair of dark-rimmed glasses. No, there was nothing that was intimidating unless you looked behind those glasses and into his eyes. There, lurking within the calm, placid deportment of a small-town politician was madness. Madness, Donovan was sure, that was put there by the influence of the Master.

"Mr. Mayor," Donovan said respectfully. "You wanted to see me?"

"Yes, Donovan," the mayor replied pleasantly. "Do come in and close the door behind you."

Donovan closed the door and was startled when the deadbolt slipped into place without his help. He looked over his shoulder at the mayor.

"I just wanted to make sure we weren't disturbed," the mayor remarked, templing his fingers as he waited for Donovan to walk across the room. "Please sit down. We have much to discuss."

115

Donovan approached the desk, but before he could sit, the mayor spoke again.

"I heard something that disappointed me, Donovan," the mayor said, slowly standing. "And you know how I hate to be disappointed."

Stopping, his hands resting on the back of the chair, Donovan replied, "Yes, sir, I do."

The mayor's face darkened, and his lips tightened in rage. "Then why the hell do you continue to disappoint me?" he shouted. With a wave of the mayor's hand, Donovan was thrown against the wall on the side of the office and held there forcefully. His cheek was crushed against the exposed brick wall and his arms and legs were immobilized.

"I don't like when people lie to me!" the mayor screamed.

Suddenly Donovan felt the searing pan of whips lashing against his back underneath his clothing. He bit back a groan and clenched his jaw as a second strike slashed his skin.

116

"I didn't lie to you," he spit out through clenched teeth.

"You called 9-1-1 about the fire at the Willoughbys," the mayor accused.

"Yes, I did," Donovan said, bracing for another hit.

"You admit to it?" the mayor asked, surprised.

"Of course, I do," Donovan said. "I had to do it. You forced my hand."

"What are you talking about, Donovan?" the mayor exclaimed. "And don't try lying, I don't have any patience left."

"You told me to retain my relationship with the Willoughbys," he gasped. "I was out at the store today, trying to get Cat to tell me what they were planning to do. When I heard about the plan, I realized that I would be the number one suspect. So, I called 9-1-1 in order to be able to verify where I was before the explosion."

"Who told you about the plan?" the mayor asked.

Donovan felt himself released from the hold against the wall. He turned around and faced the mayor. "That's not information I'm going to share," he said. "The question is, why didn't you tell me about the plan?"

"I don't have any obligation to tell you anything, young man," the mayor snapped.

"No, you don't," Donovan agreed. "But if you want this plan to work, we'd better be working as a team."

The mayor eyed him suspiciously. "Are we on the same team, Donovan?"

"Haven't I proved my loyalty to you yet?' Donovan replied. "I took care of Stoughton and the Abbotts, and I gave you the credit."

The mayor nodded. "Yes. Yes, you did," he said, rubbing his chin thoughtfully. "And you showed a great deal of wisdom and refinement in the handling of that situation."

"Even though Buck Abbott told me that the Master had chosen him for his first in command," Donovan said, watching the mayor's eyes narrow in

118

reaction. "I still did what I thought was right for the good of our coven."

"I didn't realize young Abbott had those kinds of aspirations," the mayor replied. "Wanda never mentioned that to me during our tete -tetes."

Donovan suppressed a shudder at the thought of what those meetings between Wanda and the mayor would look like. He understood very well that Wanda had no qualms in using her very obvious charms to get what she wanted. And now, she wanted power and revenge.

He shrugged. "Perhaps she didn't know," he replied. "She wasn't always at the meetings."

The mayor stared at him and then shook his head. "Why such loyalty?" he asked. "You defend her when I mention that she hasn't been honest with me and you protect her when I ask you to name the person who told you about the plan."

Donovan kept his face expressionless. "I told you that I wasn't going to mention anyone's name," he said, deciding that the mayor was fishing for information.

"That's not how I operate."

The mayor chuckled softly. "You're an honorable man, Donovan," he finally said. Then the smile left his face and he met Donovan's eyes. "And I hope your honor doesn't eventually cost you your life."

Chapter Nineteen

Donovan stepped out of the City Hall to find a very large police officer standing next to his car. *Great!* he thought, *What now?*

He hurried to the curb. "Excuse me," he said, trying to tamp down the frustration in his voice. "But my car is parked legally. It was after 4 P.M. when I parked here and the no parking restrictions only last until four."

Joseph turned and looked down at Donovan, an experience Donovan was unused to. "Are you Donovan Farrington?" he asked.

"Yes, I am," Donovan answered. "What do you…"

"I'd like to speak with you," Joseph interrupted, glancing around the area. "Privately." He paused and met Donovan's eyes. "Very privately."

"And you are?"

"Police Chief Joseph Norwalk," Joseph answered quietly. "Where would you like to meet?"

121

Out of the corner of his eye, Donovan saw the curtain move in the mayor's office on the second floor.

"Damn," he whispered. The mayor was watching their encounter.

"Write me a ticket," Donovan ordered quietly.

Joseph indiscernibly lifted his glance, then met Donovan's eyes and then pulled out his pad and started writing a ticket. He walked to the back of the car, pointing to the license plate, intimating that it was expired. Donovan followed and shook his head.

"I'm arguing with you, so you can bring me in," Donovan said, his actions and his face in direct opposition to his words.

Joseph nodded slowly. "You want to take a swing at me?" he asked. "That would end it right away."

Donovan choked back a laugh. "I may be stupid, but I'm not an idiot," Donovan replied. "No one in their right mind would believe that I'd pick a fight with you."

"What if I told you that I thought Cat Willoughby was a liar?" he asked.

Without thought, Donovan swung a fist at Joseph's chin. Joseph caught it easily and twisted Donovan's arm behind his back, pinning him to the side of his car. The pressure on his wounded back caused Donovan to grunt in pain and Joseph saw the welts through the thinness of Donovan's white shirt.

"What the hell?" he asked, astonished.

"I'll explain later," Donovan said through clenched teeth. "Just put the cuffs on me and get me out of here."

Joseph loosely put the cuffs on him, led him to his cruiser and put him in the back seat, then he climbed into the front seat and pulled away from the curb. "He saw it all," Joseph said. "The curtain closed as we pulled away."

Easily pulling his hands out of the cuffs, Donovan leaned forward and dropped them in the passenger's seat. "How well do you trust the people in your command?" Donovan asked.

Joseph shook his head. "I don't really know most of them," he said. "They seem like good officers, but I'm

123

not sure about loyalty yet." He glanced back through his rearview. "I take it that I can't take you to the hospital."

Donovan shook his head. "No, that's wouldn't be wise," he replied.

"Okay, well, then my hands are tied," Joseph said and turned the vehicle onto the highway. "There's only one place I know where I can't get answers and you can get help."

Donovan shook his head. "Don't take me there," he said. "It's not safe for them."

"Is the mayor following you?" Joseph asked.

Shaking his head, Donovan still glanced out the back window to be sure. "No, I don't think he's going that far," he said.

"But he knew you were the one who called 9-1-1," Joseph said.

"How the hell…"

"I called my dispatcher when the explosion happened after I heard the call for the fire department," he said.

"Were you there?" Donovan asked.

"I heard the dispatch and I called Hazel," he said. "She and I, er, met earlier today. The explosion occurred when we were on the phone."

"Wait! I heard there was no explosion," Donovan exclaimed. "There was nothing there when the fire department arrived."

"There wasn't," Joseph said, watching Donovan through the mirror. "By the time they arrived."

Donovan leaned forward and grabbed the front seat. "Cat!" he exclaimed. "What happened to Cat?"

"She was in the store when it happened," he replied, watching the pain come into the Donovan's eyes before he fell back against the seat.

"How is she?" he asked, his voice regretful.

"She's fine," Joseph said. "She said that she heard a voice in her mind telling her to shelter herself, so she ran into the office and hid under the desk. Not even a scratch."

Donovan glared at Joseph through the mirror. "What were you trying to prove?" he asked.

125

Joseph shrugged. "Just following a hunch," he said. "I don't know who I can trust yet."

"And now?" Donovan asked.

He met Donovan's eyes through the mirror.

"Haven't decided yet," he replied evenly. "But I'm getting a better idea."

Chapter Twenty

"You need to go to bed," Agnes said as Hazel headed towards the back door.

"I need to milk my goats," Hazel replied. "And because of Rowan and Henry, I'm feeling fine."

"I can milk your goats," Agnes countered.

Hazel chuckled. "Yeah, I remember the last time you tried to do that," she said. "It didn't end well for anyone."

Agnes tried to look offended but failed. "I figured out he was a billy before I tried to put the milkers on him," she argued.

"But not before you confused the entire herd," Hazel countered, "And had them upset for hours." She came over and hugged her mother. "Besides, I need some time with Lefty, just to calm my heart a little."

Her mom hugged her back. "That I can totally understand," she said. "Okay, use whatever shortcuts you need tonight."

Hazel leaned back in surprise. "What? My own mother suggesting I use magic for menial tasks?" she exclaimed with a grin. Then she peered out the window.

Agnes sighed and rolled her eyes. "What are you looking for?" she asked.

"Flying pigs," Hazel replied. "Didn't you always say…"

"Yes, I did," Agnes retorted. "But today is an exception to the rule."

"So, the new rule is 'before you can use magic on your chores pigs will fly, unless I change the rule," Hazel teased.

"That's exactly right," Agnes replied. "A mother's prerogative."

She kissed her mom on the cheek and walked over to the door. "Okay, I'll use short cuts," she agreed. "As long as it doesn't bother the goats."

She stepped outside in the early evening dusk and took a deep breath. The fragrance from Rowan's lavender fields calmed her spirit as she made her way across the barnyard and to the door of the barn. *It had been such a strange couple of days*, she thought, *from the trip to town to the explosion at the store. But strangest of all was Joseph Norwalk. How easily he accepted who we are, no denials or accusations – he just accepted us. And, even odder, how quickly he reacted when mom told him to carry me behind the house, so no one would see my condition. Why didn't he argue with her? Why didn't he ask more questions?*

"The answers to these and other strange questions…" she mumbled as she pushed open the barn door and then she froze. Something was wrong. It was too quiet. The goats should have been bleating for their evening meal.

She rushed forward, the pens were empty. Jumping over the wooden fence she dashed into the fenced pasture. "Good girls," she called loudly. "Good girls, come home."

She listened for an answering bleat, but didn't hear anything. Running back to the barn, she picked up a

129

metal can that had grain in it. Rattling the grain against the side of the can, she hurried outside again. "Good girls," she called. "Dinner. Good girls."

But there was no response.

She ran back into the barn, hopped onto the Gator and pulled it out of the barn. Henry and Rowan were walking back from the still room and stopped when they saw her. "Is everything okay?" Rowan asked.

Hazel nodded with a little exasperation. "The goats must have found a weakness in the fence somewhere," she said with a sigh. "They're off on an adventure somewhere. But I've got the grain bucket, so they will soon be in my control."

Henry shook his head. "I'll go with you," he said.

She laughed. "Henry, these goats have gotten out so many times, it's practically a weekly event. Nothing nefarious going on here, just a bunch of naughty goats," she argued. "Really, it's no big deal and the ride on the Gator will clear my head."

"Do you have your phone?" Rowan asked.

130

Hazel patted the pocket of her vest. "Yes, it's right here," she said. "So, if I need you, I'll call."

"What direction are you going?" Henry insisted.

Hazel rolled her eyes. "Well, if you must know, I'm going to go out towards the orchard in the high pastures. The raspberries are ripe, so they are probably eating their fill."

"Okay, you will call us?" Henry insisted.

"Yes, I will," Hazel replied. "Tell Mom I'm fine, okay?"

Rowan nodded. "Okay, I will," she said. "Be safe."

Hazel rode the Gator to the gate, hopped off, then opened the gate and rode the Gator through it. Then she locked the gate behind her, waving to Henry and Rowan. "Worry warts," she muttered with a smile, as she climbed up on the ATV.

She rode across the first pasture at high-speed and stopped at the gate on the other side, only to find it already open. She paused, and a flutter of unease went through her

131

stomach. Did she unlock the fence and forget about it? She couldn't remember walking out to the pasture. She studied it for another minute longer and almost reached for her phone. Then she shook her head. This was ridiculous, she was letting them get to her. She was not going to be paranoid on her own property.

She drove the Gator through the open gate and started to go back to lock it but realized it would be easier to herd the goats back through it if it were kept open. The sun was beginning to set, so Hazel turned on the headlights on the Gator and continued across the large pasture towards the orchard.

She held the metal feed bucket in her hand and shook it again. "Good girls," she called. "Dinner! Come on home!"

"Probably feasting on raspberries," she said, but found she couldn't bring herself to smile. Her heart was pounding in her ears and her breathing was shallow. Every shadow seemed to be menacing.

"Stop it!" she scolded herself. "You're scaring yourself."

She paused for a moment on the outside of the large apple orchard. The trees were leafed out and small fruit had started to grow on the branches. The path between the trees was wide enough for the Gator to pass through easily, but with the deepening darkness, the usually cheery apple orchard was a maze of long, twisted branches and oddly shaped silhouettes.

She began to reach for her phone once again, then stopped. "Sure," she whispered. "Ask Henry to come and save his soon-to-be little sister. I don't think so."

She revved the engine on the Gator and put it into gear, moving slowly through the orchards searching for the goats. She kept calling, but found her voice getting shakier and shakier with each try. So, finally, she gave up trying and just rattled the feed bucket.

Finally, with a sigh of relief, she drove out of the orchard and onto the clearing where the raspberry patch lay. There, alongside the patch, were the goats, all

133

gathered together in a circle. She nearly cried with relief, as she drove the Gator forward. "You girls are in such trouble," she said. "Scaring me like that."

She stopped the ATV and stepped off. "Okay, it's time to go home," she said.

Suddenly, she was grabbed from behind and her arms were pinned to her side. She twisted and fought, but whoever held her, was much stronger than she was in her weakened state.

"Let me go," she screamed.

Just then, a familiar figure stepped forward, out of the shadows of the tall raspberry bushes and walked into the beams of light from the Gator.

"Wanda," Hazel said, glaring at the woman. 'You really don't want to do this."

"Hazel dear," Wanda said. "How nice of you to join us. We decided that the Master needed a celebration, so we decided on a blood sacrifice."

"If you kill me…" Hazel warned.

Wanda laughed. "Oh, silly, I wouldn't kill you," she said, waving to another person in the group. "Come show little Willoughby our choice for tonight."

A burly man walked forward with something squirming in his arms. He too stepped into the beams of the Gator and in his arms he held Lefty.

"No!" Hazel screamed, her eyes filling with tears. "No! Don't hurt him."

She turned to Wanda. "Please, no," she pleaded. "Please, he's done nothing to you."

Wanda smiled. "Oh, dear," she mocked. "I had no idea he meant so much to you." She turned to the man holding the baby goat. "Make sure his death is painful."

Chapter Twenty-one

Rowan and Henry stepped up onto the patio steps when the police cruiser pulled in behind the house.

"I wonder what this is all about," Rowan said.

"Looks like there's someone in the back seat," Henry replied as they hurried toward the vehicle.

Joseph opened the door. "I need your help," he said. "Donovan needs some medical care and then I need to question him."

"Medical care?" Rowan asked. "What's wrong."

"The mayor was displeased that he called 9-1-1," Joseph said, then he paused and slowly looked around. "Where's Hazel?"

"The goats got out again," Rowan said. "She took the Gator up to the orchard to find them."

"In the dark? Alone?" he asked harshly. "What the hell were you thinking?"

"We..." Rowan began.

"How do I get there?" Joseph demanded.

"There's no road," Rowan stammered. "It's through the pasture, about two miles over that hill."

"Get as close as you can with your cars," Joseph demanded. "And meet me there."

"What are you going to do?" Henry asked, as Joseph jogged away from them.

Joseph looked over his shoulder, his eyes reflecting yellow in the deck light. "I'm going to run," he replied, his voice a low growl and then he dashed away from them.

Donovan ran over to them. "Get everyone, now!" he called.

"But…but Hazel said it was no big deal," Rowan insisted.

"Everything is a big deal now," Donovan said. "And right now, Hazel, one of the three necessary to stop the Master, is vulnerable."

The door opened, and Cat and Agnes ran forward toward the stairs with Fuzzy at their feet. "Hazel?" Agnes cried.

"The orchard," Rowan replied, running towards the Jeep. "Joseph wants us to take the road and come in from the other side."

As Agnes and Cat ran to meet the others at the Jeep, Fuzzy took off through the pastures, following Joseph's scent.

Joseph leapt the fence on the far end of the pasture. He picked up her scent earlier and the darkness of the night increased his other senses. He could feel the fear for her course through his body, could feel the anger towards her enemies increase his adrenaline. Then he heard her scream and he could no longer hold back the change.

He ripped his shirt over his head as he ran, his body buckled and twisted. His face altered and narrowed. His skin peeled back, and new muscle, sinew, and fur replaced it. He paused for only a moment and howled his war cry into the night sky and sprinted ahead on all four legs.

He could smell her and could hear her heart racing. He could smell the others, felt the terror from the animals and the hate from the humans. He flew through the orchard, his padded feet silent on the grass. He was only a few yards away and narrowed his sights on the one holding her.

"Please, no," Hazel begged.

"Better yet," Wanda said. "Kill him here, in front of her, so she gets to watch the consequences of her decisions."

"Wanda no!" Hazel screamed.

"Sorry, dear," Wanda said. "You chose the wrong side this time."

The loud growl echoed through the orchard and suddenly Hazel's captor was gone. Hazel reacted immediately, focusing her energy on the man holding Lefty. She held her hands apart, her fingers wide, and slowly brought them together, as if she were holding an invisible balloon. The man started to gasp, and his face turned purple. He dropped to his knees, releasing the little goat and grabbed his throat, gasping for air.

Hazel stared at him, hate running through her veins, feeling blood lust nearly overcome her. "No!" she yelled, then dropped her arms. "You aren't worth it."

The man collapsed to the ground.

She turned around to face Wanda and was surprised to see Wanda backed against a tree, her face filled with fear. Hazel turned and gasped aloud. The beast stood over six feet all. His arms were long and muscular, and his paws had claws that were at least six inches long. He was covered in fur, yet he stood like a man. His massive jaws were covered in blood and Hazel turned to see the man who had held her captive was laying bloodied on the ground.

It had saved her. Whatever it was, whoever it was, had saved her.

"Thank you," she said to the beast.

It turned to her, for only a moment, and she felt the connection to her soul.

Suddenly the pasture behind the raspberry patch filled with light as the high-beams from the Jeep flashed over the hill.

The shadows standing near the raspberry patch dispersed quickly, running in all directions. With a scream of fear, Wanda ran too, and the beast growled at her. She fell to the ground in fear, then scrambled away, through the thorn-infested berry patch, as quickly as she could. Hazel wanted to laugh and cry at the same time. She turned to thank the beast once again, but he was gone. Was he pursuing Wanda and the others?

Suddenly Fuzzy appeared at the edge of the orchard. "Fuzzy," she cried. "Go help the wolf. Go!"

Fuzzy lifted his nose up into the air to catch the scent, then turned and ran back into the orchard.

Stumbling forward, Hazel ran over to Lefty. He cuddled close to her, frightened and trembling. "It's okay, baby," she crooned. "We're going to get you home. We're going to get you home right now."

She tried to lift him, but it was too much. She couldn't get the strength to do it. Laying her head against the little goat, she sobbed into his fur.

"Hazel," Agnes called. "Hazel, where are you?"

"I'm here," she cried weakly. "Over here."

Henry got to her first and wrapped his arms around her. "Are you hurt?" he asked.

Looking up to him, her eyes filled with tears, she shook her head. "Thanks for being the cavalry."

"I shouldn't have let you go alone in the first place," he said. "If not for Joseph…"

"Joseph?" Hazel asked. "Where is Joseph?"

"He took off running to help you," Henry said, "Once he told the rest of us what to do." Then Henry chuckled softly. "But I don't think he understood how far away it was."

Hazel nodded slowly, but in her heart she knew that Joseph had arrived just in time.

Chapter Twenty-two

Standing inside the barn, leaning against the pen wall, Hazel watched the goats rush for their grain. Even Lefty seemed to be back to his usual antics, trying to grab a little grain from each separate feeder.

"Looks like they're going to be fine," Rowan said, leaning shoulder to shoulder with Hazel.

Hazel sighed and nodded. "Yes," she agreed with a sigh. "Thank goodness."

"And how about you?" Rowan asked. "How are you going to be?"

Hazel turned to her sister and smiled. "Actually, I'm better than I thought I'd be," she said. "It was terrifying for a moment. And it was really foolish of me to leave myself in a vulnerable position like that. But, I'm good."

"So, you haven't really filled us in on the details," Henry said, as he tossed fresh straw into the pen. "When is that going to happen."

"I need to get things straight in my mind," Hazel said. "And I really need to speak with Joseph to clarify things."

Henry leaned against the rake and shook his head. "I still don't know how Joseph made it there before us," he said. "And why did he disappear before we got there."

Hazel nodded. "And those are some of the things I want to talk to him about," she said. "But I really think it needs to be just the two of us, at least at first."

Rowan pushed back, away from the wall. "So, can we help you with the milking?" she asked.

Hazel shook her head. "No, but thanks. It won't take me long and I need a little time to process things," she said.

"We'd really like to help," Henry added.

Hazel laughed. "I see this for what it is," she teased. "You don't want to go inside with Mom."

"She is a little frantic," Rowan admitted.

"Well, you two need to calm her down," Hazel said, then her tone changed, and she was completely

145

serious. "And you need to find out what going on with Donovan."

"You're right," Henry agreed, coming over and putting his arm around Rowan. "Come on, sweetheart, no use hiding out in the barn any longer."

Rowan leaned over and hugged her sister. "Call if you need us," she said.

"I will," Hazel promised.

Hazel waited until they left the barn and then quickly snuck outside to the police cruiser. With a wave of her hand, she easily opened the trunk, looked inside and, with a satisfied smile, found what she was looking for. She gathered the items up and carried them back to the barn with her, awaiting Joseph's arrival.

She'd nearly finished all the milking when she sensed Joseph's nearness. The goats also seemed to sense him and then gathered together in the center of the pen for protection.

"It's okay girls," Hazel cooed. "He's our friend, he won't hurt you."

Stepping outside, she saw him quietly heading toward the cruiser with Fuzzy at his side. When he walked through the beam from the overhead light, she could see that he was shirtless and shoeless. Then he stepped toward the cruiser and was once again in the shadows.

"They're in here," she called.

He froze and slowly turned towards her. "I beg your pardon?" he asked.

She smiled and walked towards him in the darkness. "I said your change of clothes are in the barn," she replied. "I thought it would be more comfortable for you to change inside."

He stared at her for a long moment, then shook his head. "And that's it?" he asked.

She came closer until she was standing in front of him. "No, that's not it," she said softly. "Thank you. Thank you for saving me."

She could tell that he was still very confused. "No questions?" he asked. "No concerns?"

147

She shrugged. "Well, okay," she began. "What kind of creature are you?"

"Wulf folk," he replied.

"A wolf person," she said and then smiled at his surprise. "I took German in high school. I was a nerd."

He nodded slowly, searching her eyes for some kind of reaction. Then he shook his head and finally asked, "Why isn't this a surprise for you?"

Hazel shrugged. "You know, I've heard rumors about wolf people my whole life," she explained. "I've just never seen one in person."

"So, are you impressed?" he asked with a cocky grin. "Any other questions?"

She stepped forward and saw that his nose was still elongated. She reached up and gently stroked it. "Full moon?" she asked.

"No," he said, holding his head still as she caressed it. "It's not a curse, it's an ability. I can pretty much turn it on and off when I need it."

She slipped her other hand up onto his shoulder and looked into his eyes. "Housebroken?" she teased.

He chuckled softly. "Yes," he said, his voice thick. "Definitely yes."

She moved her hand, so it caressed his cheek, her eyes wide with wonder. "Fixed?" she asked with a mischievous smile.

Shaking his head in wonder, he wrapped his arms around her and pulled her against him. "Definitely not," he growled softly.

She lifted her face towards him and trembled at the intensity in his eyes. "Joseph…" she sighed.

He lowered his face and crushed his lips against hers— tasting, exploring, and possessing. She moaned and returned his passion, her hands threaded through his hair, pulling him closer. He felt the adrenaline rush, felt a different kind of heat pour through his veins. He wanted her with an intensity he'd never felt before, with a hunger he'd never experienced.

He felt her shudder in his arms and then tasted the saltiness of a tear. He leaned back and saw her, eyes brimming, lips swollen from his kisses, and her face flushed. "Hazel?" he asked tenderly.

The tears overflowed and streamed down her cheeks, she looked up at him in confusion. "I don't…" she stammered. "I never…"

He pulled her back into his arms, but his time there was comfort rather than passion. This time the soft kisses that he rained on her face were tender and sweet. This time, when she placed her head against his shoulder, he knew that she was finding comfort and security. And, he knew, that he would always want to be that place for her.

Finally, when her trembling had ceased, he looked down at her and smiled. "I probably should change," he said softly.

She ran her hand across his muscular bare chest and sighed. "I kind of like you this way," she replied, and he was relieved to see her teasing smile return.

"It's not regulation," he replied with a smile, tucking her against his side and walking with her to the barn.

She sighed. "That's too bad," she said. "You would have women from all over the area confessing to all kinds of crimes if you dressed like this."

"Well then, I'm doing it to prevent a crime wave," he chuckled.

They walked inside the barn and the goats immediately panicked. Fuzzy found a stack of haybales to climb up on, on the other side of the barn and laid down to rest.

"Fuzzy's not causing their panic, they still smell the predator side of me," Joseph said. "I'll just go in the back and change."

She handed him his clothes and pointed out a bathroom in the back of the barn. "I'll be done here by the time you get out," she replied.

He walked away, and Hazel walked the last doe up to the milking stand. She leaned her head against the doe's flank, as she adjusted the milkers, and sighed. "So, Florence," she whispered to the doe. "What am I supposed to do now? I think I'm falling in love with a wolfman."

The doe bleated sympathetically.

Hazel nodded. "You're right," she agreed. "What the hell am I thinking?"

Chapter Twenty-three

When he walked out of the bathroom, Joseph's features were all back to normal. "So, any Wulf folk visible?"

Hazel shook her head. "No, you're back to normal Chief Norwalk," she said, then she looked over her shoulder. "Even the goats aren't worried."

With his extra clothes under his arm, he walked over to the pen. "How's Lefty?" he asked.

"See for yourself," she replied softly. She pointed over to a smaller pen and they both looked over the half wall at the little goat sound asleep nestled against his mother.

"He's probably exhausted," Joseph said. "That was quite an adventure."

Hazel nodded and then turned to him. "Thank you again," she said. "For saving us both."

He looked down at her. "Don't ever put yourself in that kind of a situation again," he said firmly.

153

"After your appearance, I think Wanda is going to think twice about coming to the farm," she replied. "But, you're right, I need to remember that we're in the middle of a war."

"Speaking of that," he said, glancing over his shoulder toward the house. "Whose side of the war is Donovan on?"

Hazel shrugged. "I'd really like to believe that he's on our side," she said sadly. "But I don't know. Cat doesn't trust him, but he broke her heart several years ago, so I'm not sure she has the most objective point of view."

"I need to interview him, and the rest of your family about what's going on," he said. "I was hoping that my, um, ability…"

She nodded. "This is your secret," she said. "You have the right to decide who knows about it and who doesn't. But we do need to be sure that our stories about what happened tonight are consistent. There were a lot of people there who saw a wolfman come out of the orchard."

He nodded. "And your family knew that I ran to help you," he said, "Instead of driving with them."

"And if you hadn't," Hazel said, her voice shaking. "Lefty would not be alive right now. You arrived just at the perfect moment."

He looked down at her, his eyes clouded for a moment. "When I heard you scream," he said, "I was so afraid that I was going to be too late."

She reached up and stroked his cheek. "So, what are we going to say?" she asked.

He thought about it for a moment. "How about if we tell them that Fuzzy and I ran out of the orchard at the same time? I went for the man holding you and Fuzzy went after Wanda. Then, once you were released, you took out the man holding Lefty. When they all ran off, Fuzzy and I pursued them."

She nodded. "Then it looks like Wanda's wolfman is just Fuzzy," she agreed. "And she was overacting." She smiled at him. "It was dark enough that nothing was too clear. I think that will work."

Joseph turned to Fuzzy. "Are you okay with this story?" he asked.

Fuzzy lifted his head and yawned widely.

"Yeah, this won't be the first time Fuzzy was pulled into a little intrigue," Hazel admitted. "He's gotten me out of trouble more than once."

"Why do I have no problem believing that?" he asked with a tender smile.

"Because you are obviously an experienced law enforcement official who understands people very well," she said, then she nodded her head in the direction of the house. "We should probably go in."

He put his clothing down on a bale of hay next to the pen, then put his hands on her shoulders. "And what do we say to them about us?" he asked.

She reached up, pulled his head down for a quick, hard kiss and then released him. "I don't think we'll have to say anything," she replied. "Because they are probably all already speculating on their own."

Chapter Twenty-four

"Who is this Norwalk and what's the deal between he and Hazel?" Donovan asked when he, Cat and Agnes were all gathered together in the family room.

"Oh, nothing, dear," Agnes said. "Chief Norwalk just gave her a ticket yesterday morning. But they were able to clear up that misunderstanding."

Donovan shook his head. "No, he was going far beyond being a law enforcement officer when he found out Hazel was out in the pasture on her own," he said. "There was a lot of emotion in his reaction."

Cat shrugged. "So, what if there was?" she asked. "I really don't see that it's any concern of yours."

"I've known Hazel since she was a skinny kid with skinned knees," he said. "She's like my kid sister."

"And then you left, and she grew up," Cat said bluntly. "None of your business."

Agnes looked back and forth between the two of them and shook her head. "Let's concentrate on what's going on with the covens," she said sternly. "And then you two can work out your own personal difference after that."

"After what?" Rowan asked, entering the room with Henry.

Agnes sighed and rolled her eyes. "Can we ever have a conversation in this house without having to repeat ourselves?" she asked.

Rowan shook her head, as she and Henry headed over to sit on the couch. "No, probably not," she said easily. "Especially when you don't wait to start the conversation until everyone is here."

"Donovan was asking about the relationship between Hazel and Joseph," Cat remarked.

"I know, right?" Rowan exclaimed, smiling at Donovan. "I'd say the police chief is more than a little interested in our Hazel."

"Can we please stick to the topic?" Agnes asked.

"Sure," Rowan replied. "What's the topic?"

"The other coven and what's going on with it," Agnes ground out through clenched teeth.

Henry cleared his throat and Agnes glared at him.
"I do apologize, Agnes," he said. "But I believe there's
one more item a little more pressing. When Joseph
initially pulled up with Donovan in his cruiser, he said that
he brought Donovan here for medical attention. And, as I
can see blood seeping down the back of his shirt, I'd say
that was a priority."

Cat turned toward Donovan in astonishment.
"You're hurt?" she exclaimed, jumping up and coming
over to him. "Why didn't you say…"

She looked at his back and gasped. "Who did this
to you?"

"It doesn't matter," Donovan said. "I'm fine. It
looks worse than it is."

Henry walked over, placed his hand on Donovan's
shoulder and then shook his head. "No, actually, it feels
much worse than we can see," he replied evenly. "Take
your shirt off, Donovan."

Donovan shook his head. "I said…"

159

Hazel entered the room at that moment, waved her hand in Donovan's direction and instantly his shirt was gone. She looked at him and shrugged. "Argument's over," she said.

"Brat," he replied.

Henry looked at Donovan's back and then looked up. "Agnes, I believe some of Rowan's Calendula ointment would be helpful. Would you mind?"

Agnes shot up. "No, of course," she said. "I'll get some immediately."

Henry glanced over at Rowan meaningfully.

"Here Mom," Rowan said. "Take my keys for the still room. I just made a new batch and it will have stronger properties that the others. If you don't mind?"

"Of course, I don't mind," Agnes said.

"Take Fuzzy with you," Joseph insisted and the wolf standing at this side hurried after Agnes.

The room was silent until they heard the back door close. "Why did you want my mother out of the room?" Rowan asked.

160

Henry glanced at Rowan and then back at Donovan's back. Rowan followed Henry's gaze and her stomach turned at the sight of the raw and oozing flesh.

"Donovan," Henry said. "I need you to carefully lay down on your stomach. Joseph come over here and help me."

The two men supported Donovan as he moved into a prone position. Cat's eyes filled with tears as she saw the ragged gashes of torn skin across his back. She knelt on the floor next to Donovan's face. "Who?" she asked, her voice breaking.

He took her hand in his and brought it up next to his face. "Don't cry, sweet Catalpa," he whispered. "I've had worse."

Henry looked at the old scars on Donovan's back and met Joseph's eyes, Donovan hadn't been lying about that.

Joseph stepped away to let Rowan close and she gasped softly when she saw the damage. She looked at Henry and nodded. "Together?" she asked.

"Together," he replied.

Henry placed his hands on Donovan's back and Rowan knelt next to Henry, laying her hands over his. They both closed their eyes and Rowan spoke first,

Bind the wound and heal the skin,

Remove the ache that lies within,

Then Henry spoke,

We take the pain to us from thee,

As we ask, so mote it be.

Rowan's hands tightened over Henry's as the pain of the wounds flowed from Donovan's body into their own. Joseph watched as Henry's face grew pale and, for a moment, slashes of blood appeared on the back of his shirt. He looked over at Donovan's back and watched the skin heal, the ragged cuts bind together, and the redness dissipate.

"Henry, don't try to take it all in," Rowan gasped. "We need to share. There's black magic involved."

"I'm fine," Henry said weakly. "We're almost done."

In frustration, Rowan slid her hands from above Henry's to lay on either side and suddenly she grimaced in pain and drops of sweat beaded on her forehead.

Joseph turned to Hazel. "They're in pain," he whispered urgently.

She nodded. "All magic has a price," she whispered back. "Healers are required to take the pain of the injury into their own bodies and then release it. Part of the healing process is the sacrifice of the healer."

"But they are both sharing it," Joseph said. "Why is it so painful?"

"Because they are fighting both the injury and the black magic that caused it," Hazel said. "Filtering the dark energy out of their bodies is harder than just moving the pain and injury out."

Finally, Rowan and Henry lifted their hands from Donovan's back and sat back against coffee table, exhausted. Donovan sat up and turned to them, moving his shoulders experimentally. "You did too much," he accused gently.

163

"We did what was necessary," Rowan whispered, placing her hand on his arm. "You are my family, Donovan."

"Thank you," Donovan replied, his voice thick with emotion.

Then Rowan turned to Henry. "And you," she said, laying her forehead against his. "You took too much."

He nodded, his eyes still closed. "I thought I could handle it," he said wearily.

She kissed him softly. "You thought wrong," she whispered. "But I love you for trying to protect me."

He opened his eyes warily. "You do?" he asked.

"Yes," she said. "This once, because you thought you were protecting me. But if you try this again, I'll have Hazel turn you into a were-raccoon."

Joseph turned to Hazel in surprise. "What?" he asked.

Hazel grinned. "Old family joke," she whispered. "Really, it's nothing personal."

Chapter Twenty-five

When Agnes returned with the container of salve, everyone was comfortably seated in the great room. "Here you are, Donavan," she said, handing him the container. "Although I assume that you really won't have any need for it, now that it served its purpose to get me out of the room."

She turned to Henry. "You must learn to be a little more subtle, dear," she said.

"Englishmen are the epitome of subtlety," Henry said with a fond smile at Agnes. "You are merely wiser than your years."

Sitting in an oversized chair, Agnes looked around the gathering. "Now, how do we start?" she asked.

"If it's all the same to you, Agnes," Joseph inserted. "I would like to ask some questions, considering part of this is now a police investigation."

Agnes nodded. "Of course, please, be my guest."

Joseph turned to Donovan. "Did you meet with Mayor Bates this evening?" he asked.

Donovan nodded. "Yes, I did," he replied. "Mayor Bates sent me a text requesting a meeting."

"May I see that text?" Joseph asked.

Donovan fished his phone out of his pocket and pressed it on. Then he accessed his text application and looked down. "It's right..." he stopped and then scrolled, looking confused. "It was right here. It was the last text I received."

"Is it in your deleted file?" Cat asked.

He shook his head after he accessed the deleted folder. "No, it's not in there either," he said, then he looked up and met Joseph's eyes. "I don't have any proof that the mayor summoned me to his office this evening."

"Which is probably what he'd like," Joseph said. "But let's just say, for the moment, I believe you." He paused and studied Donovan. "Which is, in part, because I stood in front of your car waiting for you to exit City Hall

167

this evening and I saw the mayor's curtain slide open when I was speaking with you."

"Thank you for believing in me," Donovan said. "At least for the moment."

"What were you discussing with the mayor?" Joseph asked.

"He learned that I'd called 9-1-1 and reported the explosion," he said.

"Before the event," Joseph said.

Donovan nodded.

"So, a couple of questions," Joseph stated. "Why would you call 9-1-1 before the event? Who told you about the event? Why didn't you just call the Willoughbys when you found out about the event? And why did you telepathically warn Cat, if you didn't plan on telling them about the event?"

"Right!" Hazel said, turning to Donovan. "Why?"

"I learned about the event fifteen minutes before it was supposed to happen," he explained. "I called 9-1-1 because I thought if the fire department were here, at the scene as soon as it happened, they could mitigate the damage. I warned Cat telepathically because I didn't want her to get hurt."

"But why didn't you call?" Cat asked him.

He paused for a moment and then sighed. "Because I knew that they would know that I called you and there would be repercussions," he said, not meeting any of their eyes.

"Wow," Hazel said, standing up and walking away from him. "Just wow."

She walked out of the room and Joseph got up to follow her. "I'll be right back," he said softly.

Hazel was in the kitchen, her arms wrapped around her waist, staring out the window into the back yard. Joseph came up behind her and wrapped his arms around her, pulling her back against him. "Are you okay?" he asked.

"He was my big brother," she whispered, and Joseph could hear the tears in her voice. "I thought...I thought even when he went away that he was still on our side."

"We haven't heard everything yet," he reminded her. "Try to give him the benefit of the doubt."

She looked up to him, tears in her eyes and asked, "Is that what you do? Give people the benefit of the doubt?"

He smiled down at her. "Hell no," he said. "I'm law enforcement. I think everyone's guilty until they can prove otherwise."

Her eyes widened in surprise and then she clapped her hand over her mouth as laughter emerged. "That wasn't fair," she said, laughing through the tears.

"No, it wasn't," he agreed. "But really, hear him out before you judge him. Okay?"

She sighed and nodded. "Okay," she agreed, wiping her eyes with her hands.

They came back in to the room and Donovan looked up and met Hazel's eyes. She stared back at him. "Tell me, Donovan," she insisted, not breaking eye

170

contact. "Tell me that you didn't call Cat because you were afraid you'd get in trouble with the other coven."

"No, that wasn't the reason," he said evenly. "I wasn't afraid of getting in trouble."

"Did the mayor cause those welts on your back?" Joseph asked.

Donovan nodded. "Although he could testify that he never laid a hand on me," he explained. "The marks on my back were caused by the mayor."

"Why?" Joseph asked.

"Because he learned that I called 9-1-1," Donovan replied.

"And why did he let you leave?" Joseph asked.

Donovan took a deep breath and glanced over at Cat, then turned back to Joseph. "I told the mayor that I had called 9-1-1 because I needed to be able to verify my whereabouts just before the explosion," he said. "Because I had visited the store this morning, I would be suspected of setting the explosives."

"So, 9-1-1 was your alibi," Cat said sadly.

171

Donovan shook his head. "Yes," he said. "Yes, it was."

Joseph studied the man who looked as miserable as he'd ever seen anyone look in his life. "You work downtown, right?"

Donovan looked up, surprised. "Yes," he said.

"And there are a number of public places—bars, restaurants, stores, hell, even the library— where you could have gone to ensure you had a public alibi, right?" Joseph asked.

"Well…" Donovan began.

"So why would you risk calling 9-1-1 if your only motivation was to obtain an alibi?" Joseph countered.

"I didn't think of the other…" Donovan began.

"Stop," Joseph said. "So far you haven't appeared to be a stupid man, so let me rephrase my questioning. You find out 15 minutes before the event that it's going to happen. You immediately call 9-1-1 and then, somehow, you're connected with Cat and you urge her to hide. A

172

communication that will protect her, but you can hide from the coven. Right?"

"Right..." Donovan replied hesitantly.

"And then you go over to the mayor's office where he beats you mercilessly for calling 9-1-1," Joseph continued. "A call you knew he would find out about, especially if you hesitated to call Cat because you knew it would be discovered."

Donovan shook his head. "Wait," he said.

"So, what were you really protecting?" Joseph asked. "You or your cover?"

Chapter Twenty-six

Donovan stood up. "I think it's time for me to leave," he said abruptly, then walked out of the room.

Cat jumped up and ran after him. "Wait!" she called.

He stopped at the back door, his hand on the door frame. "Cat, go back into the room," he said without turning to face her.

"I want you to tell me," she demanded. "I want you to tell me who you're protecting."

He shook his head. "I can't," he said.

"Because you're protecting yourself," she cried.

He didn't say anything, just stepped outside, and walked slowly down the steps. Cat ran to the door and watched him, tears running down her cheeks. "I wanted to believe you," she whispered. "I really wanted to believe you."

Then she turned and ran up the stairs to her bedroom.

Hazel turned to Joseph. "So, what do you think now?" she asked.

He shrugged. "I don't know," he said honestly. "But I'm going to find out."

"He's not going be out there," she said. "He's going to be long gone."

"He'd better not be," Joseph said, shaking his head. "I brought him in my cruiser."

Joseph stood up and turned to Agnes. "I apologize for causing so much turmoil in your home," he said.

She smiled at him. "Oh, turmoil is second nature here," she said easily. "But I have to thank you for interrogating Donovan like that. It's given me a lot to think about."

"Me too," he agreed. "Me too."

He turned to Rowan and Henry. "It was nice meeting you."

"I'm sure we'll see you again," Rowan replied with a smile.

He glanced over at Hazel and then turned back to Rowan. "I'm sure you will too," he said decisively.

"I'll walk you out," Hazel said, linking her arm through his.

They left the great room and walked through the kitchen in silence, then they stopped at the door. Joseph turned to her. "You need to be careful," he said. "I don't want you to take any chances."

"I've locked the goats down for the night and Henry has an apartment right over them," she said. "So, they'll be safe."

"I'm glad for the goats, but they're not the target," he said. "It will take all three of you to defeat this Master. If the other coven can eliminate one of you, they win."

"Eliminate?" Hazel asked.

Joseph took Hazel's upper arms in his hands. "Think about this, Hazel," he said. "Where would Cat have been normally at 5 P.M.?"

Wide-eyed, she stared at him. "Locking up," she said. "Locking up the store."

"Right," he replied. "And where was the most damage from the explosion?"

She gasped softly, replaying the scene in her mind. "At the front of the store," she said. "It was all at the front of the store."

"Do you think these people are playing games?" he asked. "They wanted to kill her. They wanted to kill your sister. And they would have killed you too. You need to realize that this really is a war. And you need to realize that you have enemies who want you or your sisters to die."

Her face became pale and she shook her head. "I didn't..." she stammered. "I thought...it's been just a story for so long. I don't think I realized..."

"Realize it now," he said forcefully. "Realize it, and make sure the rest of your family realizes it. Because that's your first defense."

She nodded and then looked up at him. "Are you in danger now?"

He leaned down, kissed her gently and stepped back. "No more than usual," he said. "I'm going to take Donovan home now. But I'll be back in the morning. I want to walk around the store and see if I can find any forensic evidence."

"Okay," she agreed, then she placed her hand on his arm to stop him before he left. "I'm glad you're on our side."

He smiled at her. "Yeah, me too."

Chapter Twenty- seven

Hazel locked the back door and walked back into the great room where Agnes, Rowan and Henry still sat. "We need Cat down here," Hazel said, her mind awhirl with the things Joseph said to her just before he left.

"She's had a rough day," Rowan began. "Can't we..."

But Agnes, watching Hazel, shook her head. "No, Hazel's right," she said. "We need everyone together."

The soft steps on the staircase had everyone turning and watching Cat descending slowly. Her eyes were red and her face puffy from crying, but she had a determined look on her face. "I had a feeling I needed to be down here," she said. "What's up?"

Hazel took a deep breath and then looked around the room at her family. "I realized today that we could die," she said softly, her eyes filling with tears. "I mean, I know all about the legend and our part in it. I've known that all my life. But today, I realized that people want to kill us so we can't fulfill our destiny."

She shook her head. "It all seemed like just words before, something that was going to happen in the future," she continued. "But today, with the explosion and then the attack in the orchard, I realized they don't care who they kill. They just want to take out one of us, so we can't stop them."

Rowan went over to her sister and put her arms around. "Sweetie, we're all fine," she said. "We don't need to worry."

Hazel gently pushed her sister away. "See, that's what we've been thinking," she said. "But we do need to worry." She turned to Cat. "The explosion went off at 5:00 P.M. What would you be doing, what do you always do, at 5:00 P.M.?"

"I always lock the front door at 5:00 P.M.," Cat replied.

Hazel turned to Rowan and Agnes. "Do you remember how the store looked before I fixed it?" she

180

asked. "Do you remember which area had the greatest damage, with shards of glass embedded into the door and pieces of ceiling beams dropped from above?"

"Oh my," Agnes gasped, placing her hands over her mouth. "The front door. Everything was focused on the front door."

Rowan turned pale, and she stared at Hazel. "They wanted to kill Cat. These people, who have been our neighbors for years, they want to kill us."

Hazel nodded. "The kind of damage, from the beams to the glass," she said. "It wasn't a veiled threat or something to scare us. They wanted to commit murder."

"If Donovan hadn't..." Cat began, then shook her head. "I wasn't going to listen to him."

"But you did," Henry said. "And you are all safe. I agree that we need to take more precautions, that we need to start acting like we're in a war. But we can't overlook the fact that they attacked twice, and we won twice."

181

Hazel took a deep breath. "You're right, Henry," she agreed. "We did win. When we work together, when we use our abilities as a team, we win. But Joseph said something that really struck home. We need to realize that this really is a war and realize that we have enemies who want us to die. Because realizing it is our first defense."

Rowan nodded. "Okay, but what should we do next?"

"We up our game," Agnes said. "Cat, what would happen if we closed the store for a little while?"

Cat shrugged. "Well, with the kind of traffic we've been having lately," she said, "it really wouldn't affect us financially. We can pay the employees for the down time, and I can still sell products through our online store."

"Good," Agnes said. "Let's do that. I don't want customers or employees hurt in the crossfire."

She looked at Rowan. "We need weapons," she said.

"Chemical warfare?" Rowan asked, aghast.

182

Agnes shrugged. "Well, herbal welfare," she acknowledged. "Nothing fatal, just annoying—spells that will react to any kind of magic that crosses our boundaries."

Rowan grinned and nodded. "I think Henry and I could start going through Grandma's Grimoire tomorrow and see what we can come up with."

Agnes turned to Henry. "Now, Henry," she began, "about your abilities."

He nodded at her. "I need to increase my skill level," he interrupted. "I realized tonight that I bit off more than I could chew. In between helping Rowan, I'll start exploring my capabilities."

"Hazel," Agnes asked, "what do you think?"

"I think it's a start," she said. "I still need to milk the goats and take care of them, but I can also work on establishing a stronger perimeter. I need to figure out how they were able to get into the orchard without any of us knowing."

"And how they got to the goats," Henry added.

Hazel nodded. "Yeah, I need to see if they left any evidence," she agreed.

"Hazel!" Agnes exclaimed. "We just talked about—"

Hazel shook her head and smiled. "Joseph is coming back tomorrow morning to check for evidence around the store," she explained. "I'll have him walk the pasture with me and see if we can find anything back there too."

"Do we trust Joseph?" Agnes asked.

Hazel nodded. "I do," she said. "He's on our side."

Agnes turned to Cat. "Well?" she asked.

Cat smiled at her mother. "Joseph has some secrets that he's not ready to share," she said. "But he's on our side. We can trust him."

"Too bad he's not our missing link," Agnes said with a sigh.

Hazel's eyes widened, and then she quickly looked away. "Yeah," she finally said, keeping her voice even. "That is too bad."

Chapter Twenty-eight

As he walked toward the car, Joseph watched Donovan pace back and forth behind the cruiser anxiously. Finally, Donovan looked over and saw Joseph heading in his direction.

"About damn time," he muttered.

Joseph shrugged. "You could have walked."

"I could have taken your damn car," Donovan exclaimed. "But I didn't."

"Yeah, well, stealing a police car probably isn't a very smart thing to do," Joseph replied easily as he slipped into the driver's side.

Donovan sat on the passenger's side, and Joseph glanced over at him.

"What?" Donovan shouted. "You want to put me in handcuffs and make me sit in the back?"

Joseph shook his head slowly and bit back a smile. "And deny myself of your pleasant company all the way back to Whitewater? Of course not."

"Go to hell," Donovan muttered.

"See what I mean? Pleasant," Joseph chuckled as he turned the car on and put it into gear. He turned the car around and then drove to the road, making a left turn to head back to Whitewater.

About a quarter mile down the road, he looked over at Donovan, who was staring out the side window into the dark fields that surrounded the Willoughby farm. "Do you think they'll be safe?" Joseph asked, his tone now somber.

Donovan nodded. "Yeah, most of them don't have the intelligence to plan one attack, let alone multiple ones," he replied derisively.

Joseph thought about that for a moment. "Seems to me that the explosion at the store and tonight's luring of Hazel out to the orchard were pretty well planned," he replied easily. "Do they have some recruits you're not aware of?"

Donovan swung around and faced Joseph. "No, they don't," he exclaimed. "They would tell me. I'm

187

trusted. I'm one of them. I would know about any additional recruits."

"Just like they told you about the planned explosion?" Joseph asked mildly.

When Donovan didn't answer, Joseph let the quiet sink in for a few moments. Then he heard Donovan's sigh. "I don't know," Donovan finally admitted. "I don't know what they're doing anymore."

"They don't really trust you, do they?" Joseph asked.

He shook his head. "Well, they don't trust anyone," he said. "But lately, I feel their distrust for me is growing."

"You're playing a dangerous game," Joseph said.

Donovan glared at Joseph. "It's not a game, dammit," he growled. "I'm not like the Willoughbys. I'm not good or loyal or dependable. I'm selfish, I'm greedy, and I'm in it for myself."

Joseph nodded. "Which is why you saved Cat's life," Joseph replied easily. "You know, the only one you're fooling with your act is you...and maybe Cat. But that's because she's so afraid of loving you again that she's hiding from the truth."

Donovan shook his head. "You don't know me," he said. "You don't know what I've done in my life."

"You're right," he said. "But I do know that four women, four very smart and intuitive women, brought you into their lives and trusted you. They considered you a member of their family. They saw good in you and still do. And tonight, I saw at least one of them risk her life for you."

They drove in silence for a half mile, and finally Donovan sighed.

"These people, the coven, they aren't normal. They've allowed themselves to be influenced by the evil of the Master," he said, his voice low, his face staring out the windshield. "Things they wouldn't have done six months ago, they now do without a thought, without guilt, without remorse. All they want is power and influence. All they want is what the Master is whispering to them,

189

coaxing them to commit atrocities they would have rejected in the past."

He turned to Joseph. "They kill without questioning," he said vehemently. "They have bargained with their souls, and the Master has totally corrupted them. You have to understand. The Willoughbys are in more danger than they can imagine."

"And by being on the inside you can protect them?" Joseph asked.

Donovan met Joseph's eyes and nodded slowly. "Yes," he finally said. "Yes, I can."

"And what happens when you need them to trust you," Joseph asked, "in order for their lives to be saved, and they don't listen because you've been playing this game with them?"

Donavan turned away and looked out the side window. "That's a risk I'm willing to take," he said.

"Did you know that Cat almost didn't hide when she heard your voice in her head?" Joseph asked. "She almost did the opposite because she didn't know if she

could trust you."

Donovan turned back and stared at Joseph. "I

didn't..." he began.

"But that's a risk you're willing to take," Joseph

said, throwing Donovan's words back at him. He pulled

up in front of City Hall, next to Donovan's car. "You

better figure out if your game is worth it."

Donovan stepped out of the car and bent down,

looking back in at Joseph. "I'll let you know," he said.

"Yeah," Joseph replied. "Do that."

Chapter Twenty-nine

Joseph reached over to his nightstand, picked up his cell phone, looked at it and groaned. It was only 6:00 A.M. and he'd already received a text from the mayor requesting his presence in his office at 7 A.M. sharp.

He put his phone down and laid back on his pillow, looking up to his ceiling. He was really tempted to ignore the message. He wasn't required to be into the office until 8:00. Then he thought about the curtain flick the night before, and suddenly he was curious to see how the mayor was going to treat him after he picked up Donovan the night before.

He threw off the blankets and rolled out of bed. "I'm going to get up," he muttered. "But I'm not going to be happy about it."

Thirty minutes later, dressed in his uniform and with a protein shake in hand, he walked out of his apartment building and over to his cruiser. He put his hand on the door, then stopped and closed his eyes. He could hear the message from his grandfather in his mind as clearly as if he were standing next to him. "Gabriella is not well. You should come by this morning and see her."

He sighed softly, opened the vehicle and slid behind the wheel. He put his drink in the carrier and his briefcase on the passenger's seat. Then he closed his eyes and concentrated on his grandfather's face. "I have a meeting this morning at 7:00. I will arrive as soon as I can."

Once he knew his grandfather had received his message, he turned on the car and drove to City Hall. After parking the car in front of the building, he picked up his protein drink and headed up the stairs to the second floor. He strode easily to the oak door and rapped on it twice.

"Enter," came the voice from inside.

Joseph pushed the door open and walked over to the desk and took a seat across from the mayor.

"I don't believe I invited you to sit down," the mayor said, his eyebrows raised in anger.

Joseph remained seated. "You invited me to a meeting," Joseph replied easily. "But if that was a mistake, I'm happy to leave and get some other things done."

The mayor glared at him for a moment and then shook his head. "No, stay," he said. "I understand you arrested Donovan Farrington last night."

"You understand because you watched the whole thing from your window," Joseph said, picking up his drink and taking a sip.

"Why, yes. Yes, I did," the mayor replied, taken aback.

Joseph shrugged. "I get paid for paying attention to details like that," he said.

"Why did you arrest him?"

"Well, at first all I wanted to do was talk to him," Joseph said. "Seems that Farrington was the one who called in the false 9-1-1 report."

"False?" the mayor exclaimed. "What do you mean false?"

"When the fire department got there, nothing was wrong," Joseph replied, enjoying seeing the shock on the mayor's face. "No fire. No damage. Nothing."

"Then, when I asked him about it," Joseph continued, "he got a little belligerent. And, you know, I understand when folks have a bad day, but all I was trying to do was ask him a couple of routine questions. Then, when I walked behind his car, I noticed that his tags were expired. I pointed that out to him, and he took a swing at me."

He looked up and shook his head. "You just can't let assaulting a police officer go by," he said. "Once people start thinking they don't need to respect the law, why, then you've got complete chaos. So, I arrested him."

"Donovan took a swing at you?" the mayor asked.

"Surprised me too," Joseph said. "But you never know with some people."

"And what did you discover when you interviewed Donovan?" the mayor asked.

Joseph shrugged. "He admitted calling 9-1-1," he said. "Told me he got some bad information, but he'd rather err on the side of caution. I believed him."

"Then what did you do?" the mayor asked.

"Wrote him a ticket for the registration violation and drove him back here for his car," Joseph replied. "Why do you ask?"

"I was at my office for quite a while," the mayor said, eyeing Joseph suspiciously. "And when I left, Donovan's car was still here."

Joseph took another sip of his drink. "Well, I tell you, Mr. Mayor," he said. "I find when I let someone cool his heels for a little while, he's a might more cooperative when I ask him questions."

"So you kept Donovan at the station?" he asked.

Joseph smiled inwardly. *Ah, so you have a stool pigeon at the station watching my every move, do you?* he thought. *And you think you're going to catch me in a lie.*

No, sir, I didn't," Joseph replied. "I kept him with me in my cruiser while I finished some investigations I

196

had to do. I figured he was still in custody, and then I could kill two birds with one stone."

The mayor nodded slowly. "I see," he said.

Joseph stood up. "Anything else you need?" he asked.

The mayor shook his head. "No. No, that will be all."

"Have a nice day, sir," Joseph said and strode out of the room.

Once the door closed, a tall, thin, African-American man came out of a side door into the mayor's office.

"Did you hear the conversation, Kendall?" the mayor asked.

The man nodded. "He kept Donovan with him all evening," he said. "He didn't lie to you."

The mayor stared at the door Joseph had just exited. "He might not have lied," he said. "But I still don't trust him." He turned to the man. "I need you to follow him. Find out his secrets. Find out anything we can use to humble that son-of-a-bitch police chief."

Kendall nodded and walked over to the window at the front of the mayor's office. He pushed aside the curtain, pulled open the lower sash and then transformed into a crow and sailed out the window.

"Let's see just how invincible you are, Joseph Norwalk," the mayor muttered. "Everyone has their secrets."

Chapter Thirty

Once Joseph got into his cruiser, he picked up his radio and called into the station. "I'm heading out to the Willoughby Farm to follow up on the 9-1-1 call from yesterday," he said. "If I'm not in radio contact, I'll have my cell with me."

He drove out of town, passing the cut-off to County Road P that would have taken him to the Willoughby's place and continued until County Road A, closer to Wulffolk Village. He drove as fast as he could without drawing attention to himself, and soon he was on the highway with the hidden access road. He slowed his car and moved onto the shoulder to look for any other vehicles. There was nothing around him except a few crows flying overhead. "Perfect," he sighed, slipping the cruiser off the road and back behind the copse of trees.

He parked the cruiser and slipped out, locking the car behind him. Then he jogged quickly down the dirt road to the hidden entrance to the city. He pushed the

199

brush to the side and stepped into the ancient village. Running down the street, he made his way directly to the church.

"Joseph," his grandfather called, coming down the stone steps to meet him.

Joseph's stomach sank. "Is it too late?" he asked. "I came as quickly as I could."

His grandfather shook his head. "No. No, it is not too late," he said. "She is still with us, only weak."

They hurried inside the church, and Joseph ran up the stairs. He hurried down the hall to the little room and entered quickly. His breath caught as he looked down at the little girl whose skin was as pale as the pillow that nearly enveloped her head. Hurrying to her side, he knelt next to her bed and took hold of her tiny hand in his.

She turned her head and smiled wearily. "You came," she whispered.

"Of course I came," he said, holding back tears. "You are my favorite girl."

She coughed softly. "Am I going to die?" she asked him.

He gently stroked her bangs away from her forehead. "Everyone must die, schatzi," he said softly. "You know that."

"No, Joseph, that's not what I mean," she protested weakly. "Am I going to die today?"

He shook his head. "I don't want you to die today," he said. "I want you to get better."

She coughed again. "I want to get better too," she said. "But Sister Helga said there is no hope for me."

Joseph felt anger surge through him. What kind of words were those to speak to a sick child? She was not going to die. She was going to be healed.

The idea blossomed as soon as the thought went through his mind.

"Schatzi," he said, using her nickname. "I have friends. Friends who are magical. Friends who can help you get better."

"Do you?" she asked, her eyes wide with hope.

201

"Yes, I do," he said. "They are not far away, and I need to go get them. But I need you to hold on until I come back. Can you do that?"

She nodded slowly. "Will you be very long?" she asked.

He leaned forward and kissed her forehead. "No, not very long at all," he said. "I promise."

"Hurry, Joseph," Gabriella pleaded. "I want there to be hope for me."

"There is hope," he promised. "There is more than hope. There is magic."

He kissed her once more and then hurried from the bedroom. He met his grandfather in the hallway. "I'm going to get the Willoughbys," he said. "They have healers there. I'm bringing them back for Gabriella."

His grandfather nodded. "Will they come?"

"I pray they will," he said as he began to move past his grandfather. Then he stopped and turned. "And keep Sister Helga away from Gabriella until I return."

"Why?"

"She told Gabriella that there was no hope for her," Joseph said, his voice low and angry. "If that child loses hope, I will place the blame squarely on that woman."

His grandfather nodded. "I will call Sister Katrina to come and sit with Gabriella," he said. "I think it's time for Sister Helga to be reassigned to another position."

"Thank you, grandfather," Joseph said as he continued down the stairs. "I will return soon."

Chapter Thirty-one

Hazel guided the last doe from the milking stand back to the pen and then picked up the shovel to start cleaning out the soiled straw. Before she could lift her first scoop, she heard the door to Henry's apartment open, and a slightly weary Henry shuffled down to the middle of the staircase and sat down, a coffee cup clutched in his hands. His hair was sleep-tousled, and he hadn't shaved. He was dressed in grey sweatpants and a white t-shirt and, Hazel had to admit, looked adorably sexy.

"Good morning, Henry. Sleeping in today?" she asked cheerfully, glancing at him, then concentrating on the straw. "That sleep-tousled thing you've got going on is pretty sexy."

Henry blushed and shook his head. "I was up most of the night doing research," he said, his voice a little gravelly. "Something I saw last night when we came over the hill in the Jeep concerned me."

Hazel froze, shovel in hand, and looked back up to the staircase. "Saw?" she asked.

He nodded. "I was driving the Jeep, and as we came over the hill, I saw something behind you," he said. "It was tall enough to be a man, but it's shape was more of an animal, a wolf. It was bipedal—"

"It had a bike?" Hazel asked, trying to play ignorant.

"Bipedal, meaning it walks upright on two legs," Henry replied. Then he sipped some of his coffee. "Interestingly enough, this area is known to have documented cases of cryptozoological specimens similar to this. The Beast of Bray Road. The Michigan Dog-Man. All examples of lycanthropic creatures."

"Lycanthropic?" Hazel asked.

"Well, taken from the Greek you have lukos, which means wolf, and anthropos, which means man," Henry explained.

"Wolfman?" Hazel asked, shaking her head. "You saw a wolfman in the woods behind me?"

He took another long sip of coffee and sat back on the step and placed the mug to the side. "And, you know, I probably wouldn't have thought a thing about it," he finally said slowly, "if I hadn't noticed the look of surprise on Joseph's face when Rowan mentioned were-raccoons. And I might have even ignored that if I hadn't noticed the wide-eyed surprise on your face when your mother mentioned the missing link."

Hazel placed the shovel down against the pen wall and folded her arms over her chest. "You know what, Henry?" she said. "You notice way too much."

He picked up his coffee and sipped again. "Yeah, sucks to be a researcher," he said. "You're always looking for clues." He turned and met her eyes. "So, tell me."

She shook her head. "It's not my story to tell," she said.

"What's not your story to tell?" Joseph asked as he stepped into the barn.

Hazel looked at Joseph, then up at Henry and sighed. "Henry was just telling me that he thought he saw a strange creature behind me in the orchard last night," she explained. "He did research last night and discovered that it's a phenomenon common in this part of Wisconsin."

Joseph nodded. "Well, actually, Henry's interest makes my request even easier," he said. "I need your help this morning. It will involve healing."

Henry stood up. "I'll get dressed and be down in a few minutes," he said immediately. "Why don't you find Rowan?"

Hazel put down the shovel and started toward the door, but Joseph put his hand on her shoulder and stopped her. "Wait. Don't you want to know what it's about or who it's for?" he asked.

She shook her head. "No, you need help," she said. "And if we can, we will help you."

He lifted his hand and cradled her cheek for a moment. "Thank you," he said.

She placed her hand over his and smiled. "It's what we do," she said.

He followed her across the barnyard to a large, steel building back behind the store. Hazel knocked on the door and then stepped inside. The room was filled with stainless steel counters and a myriad of copper and stainless-steel machines throughout the room. "This is where Rowan creates her herbal combinations," Hazel explained.

A moment later, Rowan walked out of an office on the other side of the building and hurried towards them. "Good morning," she said. "What's up?"

"Why don't you explain?" Hazel asked Joseph.

"There is a child, a little girl, from my village who has been sick for a long time," he said. "In our village we practice the old ways, no electricity, no modern equipment…"

"No modern medicine," Rowan inserted, and Joseph nodded.

"I've been bringing in medications," he said, "trying to help. But since she's never received a diagnosis from a physician, I can only guess at symptoms and cures."

"And now?" Rowan asked.

"She's taken a turn for the worse," he explained. "I don't know if you can even help, but I had to ask."

"Of course you did," Rowan said, sliding off her lab coat and tossing it on the table next to the door. "Let's go."

"Henry's getting dressed," Hazel said. "He'll meet us by the car."

"That's it?" Joseph asked.

Hazel grinned at him. "Joseph, no matter what you might have heard," she teased, "we don't lock little children up in gingerbread houses or hand out poisoned apples."

"That's not what I meant," he said, shaking his head. "I just didn't expect all of you to be so generous."

Agnes walked out to the deck and waved at them.

"Mom," Hazel called to her. "Joseph needs our help. Someone is sick in his village."

209

"Oh, dear, is there anything I can do?" she asked.

"We're going to see what she needs," Rowan explained. "Then we'll know more."

"Just let me know," she replied. "And, considering what we talked about last night, I'll call Cat and have her work on the online orders from the house."

"Thanks, Mom," Hazel said. "That would be great."

Henry came out of the barn and hurried toward the cruiser. "Ready when you are," he said.

Joseph nodded slowly, still amazed at the willingness of the Willoughbys to help without question. Perhaps they deserved more information than he had been willing to divulge at first, but some secrets he still wasn't ready to share.

Chapter Thirty-two

Joseph pulled out onto the road and turned south,

heading through Kettle Moraine State Park. "First, I need

to tell you that the safety of our village and our people has

depended on the secrecy we've been able to maintain for

over two hundred years."

"You've been living in this area for over two

hundred years, and no one knows about you?" Henry

asked.

Joseph nodded, "A select few know about us," he

explained. "As a matter of fact, my grandfather mentioned

that one of the Willoughbys saved my father's life when

he was a boy. So, at least one of your ancestors kept our

secret."

"Where did you come from?" Henry asked.

"We came from a small village in the Bavarian

Alps," he explained. "We lived quietly there for

generations, keeping to ourselves and our traditions. But,

as the politics in Germany changed and the countryside

became more populated, we realized that we would not be able to hide our unique characteristics much longer."

"Unique characteristics?" Rowan asked.

Joseph looked through the rearview mirror and met her eyes. "We are wulf folks," he said. "Wolf people."

"Really?" she asked, her eyes shining with interest. "How cool! I've always heard rumors, but I've never actually seen one."

Joseph turned and looked at Hazel, who was smiling.

"You really don't know what to expect when you're dealing with a Willoughby," she said.

He shook his head. "No, I suppose you don't," he replied. Then he looked back at Rowan through the mirror. "No terror? No concerns? No worries?"

Rowan met his eyes and shook her head. "Joseph, all my life I've been judged by people who thought they knew who and what I was better than I did," she said. "They were generally wrong. Why would I judge you with that same criteria?"

He shook his head. "This is very unusual behavior," he said slowly.

"How do the witches you've met usually behave?" Hazel teased.

He nodded. "Okay, fair point," he agreed. "So, in order to escape persecution, the village elders decided to move to a place that we had heard about, a place that was like the meadows of Bavaria but with no people around for hundreds of miles. We packed up everything we had, booked an entire ship to transport us, and came to America."

"And have been able to hide out ever since?" Henry asked. "That's amazing."

Joseph shrugged. "Well, we haven't gone totally unnoticed," he said. "The research you did probably spoke of sightings of a beast, on Bray Road, correct?"

Henry nodded. "Yes, it did."

"Yes, occasionally one of our young villagers has too much ale and too much wanderlust," Joseph explained. "They decide to explore the area outside the village.

Luckily no one has ever been able to photograph one of us."

"But how do you hide your village from above?" Rowan asked. "With drones and crop-dusters in the area, someone is bound to see you."

"We in our village are not only shapeshifters," Joseph explained. "We also carry some of the blood of Merlin in our veins. It is not as strong as your blood, but it gives us enough ability to camouflage the village from the sky."

Hazel turned to him. "So, you are a witch too?" she asked.

"A distant relation I think would be a better term," he said. "But we have certain abilities we can still use."

"Yesterday, when you pulled into the barnyard," Henry said. "You seemed to immediately sense that something was happening to Hazel. Is that one of those abilities?"

He nodded and slid his hand over to grasp Hazel's hand for a moment. "When we have a connection to someone," he said, meeting her eyes, "we can feel their emotions."

"I admit that I was spooking myself," Hazel said. "Even before I got to the orchard."

He squeezed her hand gently and then released it. "Good thing you're not quite as cool as you appear," he said.

"So, you got to Hazel before we did?" Rowan asked.

"That's right," Henry said to Rowan. "I didn't have a chance to tell you. I saw Joseph, but I didn't know it was Joseph at the time, behind Hazel when we came over the hill in the Jeep."

"Joseph saved me and Lefty," Hazel said. "He took out the man who was holding me just before they were going to kill Lefty. Then he frightened the rest of them away."

"Which is why they were already running before we got there," Rowan said.

"But aren't you concerned that word is going to get out about you, now that you've been seen?" Henry asked.

"Fuzzy was just behind him," Hazel said. "So, we were just going to say that Fuzzy attacked and then scared them."

Henry shook his head slowly. "Some people might believe that," he said. "And since Wanda was leading the group, most of them were probably fools. But I think you need to be sure your village is aware of the possible danger from the coven."

Hazel sighed. "Yes, any friends of ours is an enemy to them."

Joseph pulled onto the shoulder and looked around. Then he drove the cruiser into the hiding place. He turned and looked at them. "I would be proud to fight your enemies," he said. "Now, if you would follow me, we need to hurry to the village."

Chapter Thirty-three

Hazel slipped out of the car and looked around but only saw a large field and woods in the distance. "How far are we running?" she asked.

"Not far," Joseph said, coming around the car to her.

"Is it like Brigadoon, hidden somewhere?" she said, gazing around again.

He smiled. "Something like that," he replied. Then he turned to Rowan and Henry. "Ready?"

"Sure, lead the way," Rowan said.

They ran down the narrow deer path, and Hazel noticed that as the path angled downwards, the grass got taller, and they slowly sunk out of sight. "This is amazing," she said as the path widened and she could run alongside Joseph. "Total optical illusion."

He nodded. "We have been cultivating the grass like that for decades," he said.

What do you do when it snows?" she asked, her question coming out in short breaths.

"We've trained the snowdrifts to lay in levels too," he said with a smile.

She sent him a look of pure skepticism, and he laughed. "No, for that we use the same kind of magic we use to hide the town from above," he said. The path ended in a small clearing, and they all stopped and caught their breath.

"Speaking of magic," Joseph continued, "the power used to hide the village is not an ability that all townsfolk have. It is for the high priest, my grandfather, and then passed down through his line. The people here have led sheltered lives, and many believe in old superstitions."

Hazel eyed him. "Like kill the witch?" she asked.

He nodded slowly, looking at Hazel. "They believe in healers," he said. "So, we don't have a problem there…"

"But you don't want me raining down puppies and kittens in the middle of the town square," she interrupted.

"Pretty much," he said.

"No problem," she said with an understanding smile. "I'll be on my best behavior."

He stepped forward and pushed aside a thick bush. "Welcome to Wulffolk," he said.

They stepped past him through a dense grove and then out the other side to see the beautiful Alpine village before them.

"It's gorgeous," Rowan said. "It's like a fairytale city."

Joseph nodded. "You can see the steeple of the church, just a half-mile from here," he explained. "That's where Gabriella's sick room is."

"Lead the way," Henry said. "And we'll follow."

Joseph jogged ahead, leading them onto the cobblestone street, and then hurried them through the town square and towards the church. Many of the

219

townspeople, dressed in traditional Bavarian clothing, stared at them as they ran alongside Joseph.

Hazel glanced around, smiling as she ran past the gawkers. "We could have dressed differently," she said. "If that would have helped."

"Thank you," he said. "But what you are wearing is not important. Getting you to Gabriella is."

The large oak doors to the church opened when they were only a few yards away, and a tall, distinguished-looking, older man stepped out. "I see you brought them," he said with a sigh of relief. "Thank you, Willoughbys. I am Henrich Norwalk, Joseph's grandfather, and we are very grateful."

"Don't thank us yet," Rowan said as she ran up the stairs. "Let us see what we can do."

They walked through the doors and entered the chapel, with its wooden seats, ornate, cut-glass windows, carved wooden statues and twenty-foot, domed ceiling. "The staircase is through here," Joseph said, leading them through the chapel to the other side of the church.

Hazel stared at the masterfully carved arches that held up the ceiling. "It's beautiful," she whispered.

"Thank you," Henrich said. "There is a lot of tradition built into this church."

She looked across the room and saw two carved angels hanging above the altar.

Henrich followed her eyes. "Angels warned our people to move away from Germany," he said. "They told us that we would no longer be safe there. So, we give them a special place of honor in our chapel."

She smiled at him and nodded. "I'm sure they would be pleased."

They reached the narrow staircase. Joseph led the way, followed immediately by Rowan and Henry, with Hazel and Henrich taking up the end.

They hurried down the hall, and Joseph pushed the door open quickly. Gabriella lay in the bed, her face pale and wan. Rowan moved past him and laid her hands on the little girl's neck.

"Is she…" Joseph asked, despair in his voice.

"No," Rowan whispered. "She's still with us, but barely."

Henry knelt down next to Rowan. "What do you want me to do?" he asked.

"I need to find out what we're dealing with," Rowan said. "Then we can figure out a plan." She looked up at Hazel. "I might need some of my herbs."

Hazel nodded. "I can be discreet," she said.

Rowan smiled at her sister, then closed her eyes and, with her mind, traveled through the little girl's body. "Brain and nervous system are functioning," she whispered. "Lungs are working. Heart is strong, and there doesn't seem to be any damage on it. Stomach is tiny. She hasn't been eating. Liver. Oh, my, her liver is in really bad shape and her kidneys are not much better."

"Why?" Hazel asked, leaning over the child. "Look closer. Is there a blockage?"

Rowan nodded and explored the small organ, shaking her head. "No blockage," she said slowly. "But there are spots that are dark and shriveled."

She opened her eyes and looked at Hazel. "I'll need milk thistle," she said.

Hazel stepped into the corner of the room and reached behind her back, pulling out a small brown bottle and handing it to Rowan. "Good thing I brought it along with me," she improvised.

"You don't have to hide your abilities from my grandfather," Joseph explained. "He understands who you are and how you can help."

Hazel smiled at Henrich. "Good," she said. "Thank you."

Rowan opened the bottle and took a gulp and then handed it to Henry, who did the same.

"Why are they drinking it?" Henrich asked.

"Because they are going to take the illness out of Gabriella and bring it into their own bodies," Hazel explained. "The milk thistle will help protect their organs from whatever it is that caused this."

Rowan looked over at Henry. "Are you ready?" she asked.

223

He leaned over, placed a kiss on her lips, and nodded. "Now I'm ready."

Henry spoke first:

To heal the body and remove the stain,

To calm the fear and erase the pain,

Then Rowan finished:

We willingly take the pain from thee.

As we ask, so mote it be.

Henry placed his hands over Rowan's, and they both closed their eyes and concentrated on healing the child's liver. Joseph touched Hazel's hand and motioned for her to step outside the room. After glancing over at her sister and seeing that she was fine, she nodded and stepped into the hallway.

"What would cause liver damage?" he asked.

"Well, since Rowan didn't find blockage or tumors, I would say that it was an environmental source," Hazel explained.

"Environmental?" he asked.

"She was poisoned," Hazel replied.

Chapter Thirty-four

Hazel pulled out her phone and glanced at the time. Rowan and Henry had been working on Gabriella for thirty minutes. If they didn't rest for at least a little while, Hazel was concerned they could damage their own bodies. She was about to say something when Rowan sighed and opened her eyes.

She looked up at Joseph and smiled. "She's out of the woods," she breathed softly. "But we still have some work to do."

"What did you find?" he asked. "Could you tell…"

"As we pulled it from her body into ours," Henry said, "I received a bitter taste in my mouth. So, I believe whatever caused this was ingested."

"Is she able to talk?" Joseph asked.

Just then, Gabriella opened her eyes and smiled up at Joseph. "Joseph," she exclaimed, her voice stronger. "You came back."

Hazel moved back so Joseph could get to the little girl. "I did," he said, his voice thick with emotion. "I came back, and I brought my friends."

Gabriella turned and smiled at Rowan and Henry. "I saw you in my dreams," she said. "You were making me all better. You took the pain away."

Rowan reached over and stroked the child's cheek. "You were very brave, sweetheart," she said. "And we have a little more to do, but we want you to rest for a little bit and drink a little of this medicine."

The little girl winced. "Please, not medicine," she said. "It always hurts my stomach when I have to take it."

Rowan shot Hazel a concerned glance. "How does it hurt your stomach, sweetheart?"

"It tastes sour, and then it makes me have cramps in my stomach," she said.

"Well, this medicine is my special medicine that won't make that happen to you," she said, opening the bottle. "Here, why don't you smell it?"

227

Very hesitantly, the child drew forward and sniffed the opened bottle. Her eyes widened in surprise. Then she sniffed it again. "It smells like honey."

Rowan nodded. "It has honey and lavender and milk thistle in it," she explained. "I call it fairy tea because I'm sure that's what the fairies must drink when it's tea time."

"Fairy tea?" Gabriella asked in wonder. "Not medicine."

Joseph laughed. "No, not medicine at all," he said. "Fairy tea. And now will you take some?"

Hazel started to move toward the bed when she caught a movement out of the corner of her eye. A woman, obviously a townsperson, had been coming toward the bedroom with a bottle in her hand, but when she heard noises, she quickly turned away.

There was something furtive in the woman's approach and more than a little suspicious in her quick departure. Hazel quietly slipped out of the room and walked to the end of the hall. She watched the woman go down the rest of the stairs and then go back behind the staircase. Moving stealthily, Hazel followed her down and moved behind the staircase to find a small door.

Pushing it open, Hazel found a path that led to a number of cottages behind the church. She glanced around and saw the woman running toward one of them. Slipping out the door, Hazel followed the woman to the last cottage on the small dirt road.

Hazel paused at the door that was wide open and heard crashing coming from within. She stepped into the cottage and watched the woman opening bottles and frantically draining them down her sink.

"Getting rid of the evidence?" Hazel asked mildly.

The woman turned and stared. "Who are you?" she asked.

Hazel shrugged. "Just an outsider brought in to save the life of the child you were poisoning," she replied.

The look on the woman's face was enough of a confession for Hazel. "Well, you can't prove anything," the woman sneered. "This is the last bottle, and it's—"

The woman yelped when the bottle was magically pulled from her hand into Hazel's grip.

"Sorry," Hazel said. "I needed it for evidence."

"You don't know who you are dealing with," the woman said.

"Same goes," Hazel replied.

Suddenly, the woman growled low in her throat, and she bent her head back while her body convulsed and shuddered. Hazel watched in shocked awe as skin was replaced by fur and muscle and fangs and claws replaced teeth and fingernails. The wolf woman towered over Hazel and glared at her with yellow eyes.

"Impressive," Hazel said, swallowing audibly. "And fairly freaky."

The wolf woman charged Hazel. Hazel swung her arm across her body and toward the creature. "Bad dog!" she cried out.

Immediately, a thick leather muzzle encompassed the wolf woman's snout and head. She stumbled back, confused.

"See, there's that same goes thing," Hazel said, "that you didn't even pay attention to."

Then Hazel waved her hand again, and the woman's claws were bound in rope. The wolf woman looked down at the rope and then up at Hazel, rage in her eyes.

"Okay, one more thing," Hazel said. "To complete your ensemble." She waved her hand at the wolf woman. "Cone of shame."

An opaque plastic collar that was about eighteen inches tall appeared on the woman's throat.

"See, that makes it a little harder for you to untie yourself," Hazel explained. She nodded. "Okay then. It was nice to meet you. I've got to go."

She heard the howl of anger as she stepped outside. Then she waited, outside the door, to hear claws scrambling across the wooden floor. At just the right time, she slammed the door shut. Hazel heard the muffled thump and the whimper. "Ouch, that had to hurt," she said and then, with the bottle in hand, jogged back to the church.

Chapter Thirty-five

Hazel ran back to the church and slipped through the small door that she'd left slightly ajar. She turned and bolted the door behind her. "Just in case wolf woman decides to come looking for me," she said to herself.

As she ran up the staircase, she saw Joseph at the top of the stairs. "Where did you go?" he asked.

"I had a little run-in with one of your townspeople," she said, hurrying up the steps. "And I think I found the poison."

"What?" he asked. "Who?"

"I don't know her name," she said as she reached the second floor and handed him the bottle. "But I saw a woman coming down the hall with a bottle in her hand. When she heard voices from Gabriella's room, she quickly turned around and hurried down the stairs."

They both walked down the hallway back to the room.

"When I followed her back to her cabin, I saw her pouring bottles of this down her drain," Hazel continued. "So, I decided to save this last one for us."

"May I have it?" Henry asked.

Joseph handed Henry the bottle, and Henry opened it, smelled it, then dabbed his finger on the edge and tasted a tiny sample. "This is what I tasted," he said.

"What is it?" Rowan asked, taking the bottle from Henry. She also smelled it and tasted a minute amount. "It's rue!"

"Rue?" Hazel asked. "But isn't that okay?"

"Not if it's used fresh or in large amounts," Rowan said, shaking her head. "And this medicine has a large amount of rue oil in it."

Gabriella looked at the bottle. "That's Sister Helga's medicine," she said. "I can smell it from here."

"Sister Helga gave you this?" Joseph asked.

"She made me take it," Gabriella said. "She told me that it would make me better."

Joseph turned to his grandfather. "If she did this…"

Henrich nodded. "We are going to have to deal with her."

Hazel sighed and looked at Joseph. "About that," she began.

Suddenly there was a commotion from outside. Joseph went to the window and opened it up.

"Witch! Witch! Witch!" came the chant from outside.

"Well, damn," Hazel muttered.

Joseph turned to Hazel. "What?"

"Okay, I may have used magic," she admitted. "But only for self-defense."

He looked back out the window. A crowd was gathering together, holding torches and pitchforks. From the back came Helga, still wearing the cone around her neck and the muzzle over her face.

"What's Helga wearing?" Joseph asked.

235

Hazel peered around him at the crowd. "Oh, well, that would be a muzzle and a cone of shame," she replied. "She really was acting like a bad dog."

Joseph turned to Hazel in amazement. "This is not a laughing matter," he said. "Do you know what they did to witches in the old country?"

Hazel rolled her eyes. "Do you really think those were witches they did that to?" she asked. "Really?"

Henrich shook his head. "What are we going to do?" he asked. "We will have a riot on our hands if we don't give them some kind of explanation. We need a miracle."

Hazel turned and smiled at him. "That's perfect," she said, hurrying to the door. "Okay, you all stay here. I have an idea."

"I'm going with you," Joseph insisted.

She sighed and rolled her eyes. "Fine, but you need to stay in the background."

She hurried down the stairs and then out into the chapel. As she walked down the large center aisle, she waved her hand, and both doors opened wide. "Angelus," she whispered.

Suddenly her clothing was transformed into long robes of white and gold, and large, white wings were attached to her back. She stepped out of the church and faced the crowd. Her long, chestnut hair was flowing freely. A golden halo hovered above her head, and her wings were outstretched.

She lifted her arms and hovered above the steps of the church.

"Good people of Wulffolk," she said in her best English accent. "We have heard your prayers of faith for the healing of your own little Gabriella."

Rowan, looking down from the window, shook her head and smiled. "She did this every year at Christmastime," she said. "She loves being an angel."

"Yeah, but will they buy it?" Henry asked, looking over her shoulder. "Her English accent is atrocious."

Suddenly, Helga ran forward with a pitchfork.

"She's a witch!" she screamed. "We need to kill her! She's a witch!"

"My sweet, confused child," Hazel said. "As you can see, I am not a witch, but an angel."

The townsfolk dropped their weapons and knelt on the ground, their faces bent.

"Looks like she convinced them," Henry said.

"Please, my good friends, please arise and be wary," she said. "We heard your prayers. And we are concerned about the innocents in your town, because there is one among you who is poisoning them."

"Poison?" the crowd gasped.

Hazel slowly lowered herself to the steps of the church and looked directly at Helga. "It is written that confession is good for the soul, Sister Helga," she said.

The crowd gasped.

"She's lying!" Helga screamed, slowly backing away from the rest of the townspeople. "She's lying. She's not an angel. She's a witch."

238

"And yet, I'm standing on hallowed ground," Hazel countered. "Why did you poison the children with rue, Sister Helga?"

"I saw her gathering rue just the other day," one townswoman cried out.

"She's a murderer!" one of the older men yelled.

Changing back into her wolf form, Helga sprinted away from the square and to the edge of town. Then she disappeared through the hedge at the border. Other townsfolk began to change too until Joseph stepped forward. "Wait," he called. "I will find Helga and we will let the laws of our country deal with her. For now, you should go back to your homes and give thanks that Gabriella is going to live."

As the townspeople started to disperse, Joseph discreetly grabbed hold of the back of Hazel's robe and pulled her back into the church. Once inside, he closed and locked the doors. Then he just stared at her.

"What?" she asked.

He stepped forward, cupped her face in his hands and whispered, "This!" And then he kissed her.

She slipped her arms around his neck and enveloped them both in her wings as she returned his kiss. Finally, they slowly separated, their breathing unsteady. "I've never kissed an angel before," he whispered, sliding his lips over hers once more.

She sighed softly. "How did you like it?" she asked, her eyes filled with love.

"It's something I could definitely get used to," he replied softly, tenderly kissing her again. Then he smiled into her eyes. "But I still think I prefer sassy witches. Even when they cause chaos and unrest wherever they go."

She grinned. "At least I'm not boring."

He laughed out loud. "No, never that."

She rested her head against his chest. "We should probably look through her cabin to see if there's anything else relevant there," she said.

He nodded, held her close for another moment, and then released her. "Okay," he agreed. "Back to reality."

As she stepped back, her wings disappeared, and her long robes were replaced by jeans and a shirt. "Back to normal," she said.

He shook his head. "You will never be merely normal," he replied.

She grinned. "Yeah, that's what my family's been telling me for years."

Chapter Thirty-six

The crow flew over the area again, searching for the small group of people. He had followed them from the Willoughby Farm and had watched them park the car and start walking through the field. He'd circled several times, keeping watch on their whereabouts, but when he made his final turn, they had all disappeared.

He flew lower, flying just above the tops of the grasses, but he couldn't see them. He tried again, flying even lower, following the path below the grass line. Suddenly the path ended, and he pulled up, flapping his wings to avoid hitting the thick brush ahead of him.

He dropped to the ground in front of the brush and noticed that the path seemed to continue into the vegetation. He hopped up to a small branch and tried to peer inside the foliage. Was there something moving in there?

Helga slashed at the deep brush, trying to find her way out of the village. She'd never come this way before, had always stayed within the safe confines of the village.

But now, because of that witch, she was forced to abandon

her home and her dreams. Damn them! Damn them all—

but especially that witch.

Like a machete, her claws raked across the brush,

creating a narrow opening that she could push through.

The collar around her neck was her greatest hindrance,

constantly getting stuck on limbs and branches and

yanking her head backwards. Growling, she swiped at the

plastic monstrosity, but it just sprung back into place,

slapping her across her snout. She growled again, her

temper flaring. As soon as she got away, she would take

care of the collar first thing.

Thrashing forward, she was making slow but

steady progress. Finally, she peered through the leaves and

could see the field beyond. She was only a yard or so

away from freedom. Just then a crow alighted on one of

the branches on the outermost part of the brush. This time

it was Helga's stomach that growled, and her mouth

watered. She'd been so busy she hadn't bothered to eat

anything that morning. Although crow would be more

bones than meat, it would satiate her hunger until she

could hunt something more substantial.

She slowly positioned herself in the brush,

knowing how far she could leap through the small window

into the boughs. She waited until the crow turned toward

the open field, and then, pushing with the mighty muscles

in her back legs, she bounded forward toward the

unsuspecting bird.

Her head soared through the shrubbery, but the

cone of shame caught on a thick, low-hanging branch. She

was jerked sideways, which changed the angle of her

attack. She tried to slow down, but the power of her

launch was too strong for her to be able to stop. She

tumbled out of the brush and fell to the ground, landing

with a thump.

"I beg your pardon!" an outraged, muffled voice

sounded from underneath her.

Helga lifted her head to find Kendall pinned

underneath her. He looked up at her, and his eyes widened

in shock. He screamed and tried to scramble out from under her, but her clawed paw held him tight.

"Who are you?" she growled. "And what are you doing here?"

Scared beyond the ability to deceive, Kendall shook his head. "I'm following Norwalk and those Willoughbys," he said.

Helga angled her head and stared at him with her yellow eyes. "Are you friend or foe of the Willoughbys?" she asked.

"Those damn witches have caused me nothing but trouble since I've been in Whitewater," he raged. "We'd all be better off without them."

She stood up, towering over him, and then smiled. "I think we could perhaps be helpful to each other," she offered.

He scrambled to his feet and quickly backed up several feet. "What are you?" he asked.

She shifted back to her human form. "No more than you," she replied. "Only more powerful."

He looked at the plastic collar around her neck and the loose muzzle on her face. "Willoughby work?" he asked.

Surprised, she nodded. "How did you know?" she asked.

"Seems like their sense of humor," he said. He waved his hand, and the objects vanished.

Helga lifted her hand to her neck and, feeling it empty, nodded her thanks. "What is it that you need to find out about Norwalk?" she asked.

"I need to discover his secrets," Kendall said.

Helga smiled slowly. "Well, you've come to the right place."

Chapter Thirty-seven

Hazel and Joseph went back up to Gabriella's room and found the others waiting for them. When they entered the room, Henrich immediately turned to his grandson. "Joseph, I must speak with you in private for a moment," he said insistently. He turned to the others in the room and nodded politely. "If you will excuse us please."

"Of course," Hazel replied. "We'll wait here for you."

Henrich closed the door behind them, which left Rowan, Henry and Hazel in the small bedroom with the sleeping Gabriella.

"I was impressed with your angel," Rowan said with a smile. "Quick thinking."

"Well, I really didn't feel like being burned at a stake today," Hazel replied, sitting on a wooden chair in the corner of the room. "I mean, it's been a really good hair day, and I would hate to waste it with a fire."

"Good point," Rowan laughed.

Hazel looked over at Gabriella. "How's she doing?"

"Good," Rowan said, her eyes gentling as they looked at the child. "She chatted with us for a little while. Then she just wore herself out. But her vitals are all good, and I think we got all of the poison out."

"You know what's weird?" Henry asked suddenly, interrupting their conversation. He'd been quietly sitting in the corner, musing over some problem for quite some time.

The girls smiled at each other. "No, professor," Hazel replied. "What's weird?"

"There aren't a lot of men in this village," he said slowly.

"What?" Hazel asked.

Henry shrugged. "As an anthropologist, it's kind of second nature to notice demographics—age, population, genders— and while I was studying that crowd out there, there were at least fifteen women to every one man. And the men were mostly older."

"Lucky men," Hazel teased.

Henry shook his head. "No, not lucky men," he said. "I looked at the children down there, and they seemed to be fairly evenly divided between boys and girls."

"So, something happens to the men at some point in their lives to make them leave the village?" Rowan asked.

"Make them leave," Henry said, meeting her eyes. "One way or the other."

"Are you talking about a disease?" Hazel asked. "Do you think the men died?"

"I don't know yet," he said. "But I think there are more secrets to this town than just wolf people."

Chapter Thirty-eight

Henrich and Joseph walked to the other end of the hallway where Henrich opened a wooden door into a small study. "Please, go in," he requested.

Joseph went in and sat in one of the small, leather chairs that flanked a small, unlit, wood burning stove. "What is it, grandfather?"

Henrich sat down across from Joseph and studied the young man's face for a few moments. Then he sighed and leaned back in the chair. "I went downstairs," he said slowly, "to see if I could be of help with the villagers. I saw you and Miss Willoughby."

Joseph straightened in the chair. "You saw us?"

"I saw you kiss her," Henrich clarified. "And I saw her kiss you back."

Joseph nodded. "A kiss is not a sin, grandfather," he said.

"But a lie is," Henrich replied. "Even a lie of omission."

"I'm not lying to her," Joseph argued, dropping his eyes to look at the floor.

"If you cannot be honest with me," Henrich said, "at least be honest with yourself."

Joseph looked up, his eyes filled with regret. "She makes me feel…" he began. "I have never met someone…"

"You sound like your father," Henrich said with a sad sigh.

"My mother was my father's great love," Joseph said, defending his parents.

Henrich nodded slowly. "I will not argue with that," he said. "But your father was not truthful with your mother. If he had been, there would have been less pain in the end."

Joseph stood up and walked to the window that looked over the back of the village. "He didn't know if she would stay with him if he told her the truth," he said quietly.

"He did not trust their love enough," Henrich argued.

"Perhaps he didn't," Joseph agreed. "But perhaps he thought that even a few days with her would be enough for both of them."

"He should have told her," Henrich said firmly. "He should have let her make her own choice. Just as you need to tell Hazel."

Joseph whirled around. "But I might not carry that gene," he said. "It may not even be an issue. Why should I bring it up when I'm probably fine?"

Henrich stood up and walked over to his grandson, placing his hand on Joseph's shoulder. "You should tell her because secrets destroy a relationship," he said. "And you should tell her because you trust her."

Joseph shook his head. "I don't even know if this relationship is—"

"Don't lie to me, boy," Henrich interrupted sharply. Then he softened his tone. "And don't lie to yourself. I have never seen you like this."

252

Joseph sighed and nodded. "I have never felt like this, and I don't know what I would do if she walked away."

"You don't give her enough credit," Henrich said. "This Hazel Willoughby is not a shrinking violet who would run away when things get hard."

"But if I do carry the gene, what woman wants to tie herself to a man like me?" he asked regretfully.

"A woman who understands that a great love only comes around once in a lifetime." Henrich replied. "And is willing to sacrifice for that love, even if it is only for a short amount of time."

"Days," Joseph said, turning away and looking back out the window. "If I carry the trait, I only have days left."

"Who can guarantee their future?" Henrich asked. "You are a police officer. She knows the danger of your job, and yet, I do not see her pulling away from you."

"But with my job, although uncertain, the odds are that I will come home," he said. "With this, the odds are high that we will only have a few days together."

"Shouldn't that be her choice, either way?" Henrich asked. "Shouldn't she have a chance to choose happiness, even if it's only for a short period of time?"

"Maybe," he said softly. "Or maybe I need to stop the relationship now, before either of us gets hurt."

"I'm afraid you may already be too late for that," Henrich said.

Joseph continued to stare, unseeing, out the window, and Henrich closed his eyes in grief. "I will leave you to think about your decision," Henrich finally said.

Joseph nodded. "Thank you," he said, his voice tight. "Please let them know I will be back soon."

Chapter Thirty-nine

Henry picked up an old, leather-bound book that lay on a shelf in Helga's home. He carefully opened the book and studied the title page. Rowan peered over his shoulder and realized that the text was in a foreign language. "German?" she asked her fiancé.

He shook his head quickly. "No, it's not," he replied, studying the words. "But it's not Latin either."

Henrich walked over to them and also looked at the book. "It is Althochdeutsch, Old High German," Henrich explained. "This book dates back to the ninth century, and it has been missing from the church's library for quite some time."

"It's beautiful," Henry said, examining the hand-painted lettering and the delicate linen pages. "It belongs in a museum."

Henrich chuckled. "Most of what we have in my library would, as you say, belong in a museum," he said.

"But they are texts for education, for passing down the old ways to the next generation."

Rowan gently caressed the old leather cover. "It reminds me of my grandmother's Grimoire," she said.

"That is not surprising. It is a book of the healing arts handed down from wise woman to wise woman in our village," Henrich replied. "Your grandmother studied this book often. Her healing arts helped many in our village."

Rowan shook her head. "She never said anything," she said.

"She promised that she would keep our secrets," Henrich replied.

Henry carefully turned page after page, scanning the words. "This is incredible," he said. "Would you mind if we studied it? There are potions in here that I've never heard of."

"It would be my honor to allow you to study it," Henrich said. "I fear that it was put to poor use by Helga. It would be good to have it used by those who seek to help, not harm."

"Do you think she used the potions in that book to make her poison?" Hazel asked as she sorted through a shelf on the other side of the room.

Henry flipped over another page. "This book shows the properties of different plants," he said. "I don't know if there was a potion or just information on the dangers of certain herbs."

Hazel pulled down a bottle from a shelf, opened it and sniffed. "This stuff is disgusting," she said, wrinkling her nose. "But I still don't understand why she did it. It's not like she would gain anything from killing Gabriella."

Joseph looked up from a journal he was reading at Helga's desk. "I'm afraid it was more than Gabriella," he said sadly. "Helga has been poisoning children for at least three years. It looks like she caused the deaths of four of the children in the village."

"Why?" Hazel asked, walking over to him. "What is her motive?"

He handed her the journal and shrugged. "I have no idea," he said. "Perhaps you can see something I have not."

Instead of looking at the later entries, Hazel immediately turned to the front of the book. She saw the initial entries were dated four years earlier. She flipped through page after page until one entry caught her attention.

Joseph came to the village to visit today. He brought toys and games for the children. He pays so much attention to them, especially to those who are weaker than the rest. How I long to have him pay that kind of attention to me.

"Bingo," she whispered, flipping forward in the book and studying more entries. "I think I might have found a motive."

"What?" Joseph asked. "What did you find?"

"Have you ever heard of Munchausen syndrome?" she asked, looking over at Henry for confirmation.

"Munchausen syndrome," Henry repeated, nodding in affirmation. "Yes, that makes a lot of sense."

"Isn't that when people fake symptoms of illnesses to get attention?" Joseph asked.

"Yes," Henry replied. "But there is also Munchausen syndrome by proxy, and it's often found in caretakers who cause children to be sick in order to gain attention."

"You're saying that Helga poisoned the children so people in the town would pay attention to her?" Joseph asked.

Hazel shook her head. "No, she didn't want the town's attention," she said gently. "She wanted your attention."

"What?" he exclaimed, standing up and looking over Hazel's shoulder to the journal. "Where does it say that?"

"This first entry where she talks about your attention to the children, especially the weak ones, concerned me," Hazel pointed out. "But, if you'll see

259

further on, she talks about how you praised her as she cared for the patients. Look at what she wrote here, *"Joseph took my hand in his today as we cared for Peter. I felt his attraction to me in his words and his touch. I know that he longs to confess his desire for me, but perhaps he waits until my time is my own. Tomorrow I will double Peter's doses, and soon Joseph will be able to ask for my hand in marriage."*

"I did no such thing," Joseph said, his grief thick in his voice. "I never encouraged...I never even thought..." He shook his head. "She killed these children because of me."

Hazel put her hand on his arm. "No," she said firmly. "She killed these children because she is mentally ill. You had nothing to do with it. You were just the focus of her fantasy."

"But if I had only known," he said, overwhelmed with guilt.

"If you had known, you would have stopped it sooner," Hazel said. "But no one knew. Even the people in the village who saw her interacting with the children day after day did not know. You can't read minds. You are not responsible."

Joseph looked across the room at his grandfather. "I should have never come back here," he said. "I'm so sorry, grandfather. I brought this community so much pain."

"Miss Willoughby is correct," Henrich said. "If it were not you, it would have been some other man."

"There were no other men, grandfather," Joseph replied.

"And that is a cross that I must bear," Henrich said. "Your father told me that we needed to bring outsiders into our community. He told me that our people were sickening because of our isolation. I was afraid."

"Perhaps we should leave you two alone," Rowan suggested. "And then you can speak freely."

Joseph shook his head. "No, there is no need for any more talk," he said bitterly. "The lot is cast, and now we must live with the consequences. Come, I'll drive you home."

"Please, take the book with you," Henrich said to Henry. "Perhaps it will do some good."

"Thank you," Henry replied. "I'll keep it safe."

Henrich nodded. "Thank you," he said. "For saving Gabriella."

Chapter Forty

The insistent rapping on his door did nothing to improve Mayor Bates' already sour mood. He had met earlier with his city council and had not been able to persuade them to fire the new police chief. Even though he had insisted that Norwalk had been insubordinate and lacking in decorum, they insisted that he was the best qualified for the job, and they had seen a decrease in response time and an increase of discipline of the force since he'd come on board.

He was composing a scathing letter to an alderman he'd helped get elected when he was once again interrupted by a knock on his door.

"What the hell?" he muttered, slamming his keyboard down on the desk, He glared at the door and finally called, "Come in."

When Kendall appeared in the doorway, Bates' anger soared. "What the hell are you doing interrupting me in the middle of the day?" he shouted.

Kendall continued into the room, and Bates saw that he had someone with him. "Who the hell is with you, and why is she dressed like an Oktoberfest whore?"

A low growl emanated from the woman, and Bates quickly stood up and slid behind his chair. "What the hell is going on, Kendall?" he asked.

Kendall quickly shut the door and then turned to Bates. "Mr. Mayor, I'd like to introduce you to Helga Dordrecht. She is from the same village as Joseph Norwalk. Miss Dordrecht, this is our mayor, Edgar Bates."

The mayor studied the young woman, then finally smiled and nodded. "Miss Dordrecht."

She curtsied quickly. "Mayor Bates," she replied.

"Why are you dressed in that costume?" he asked.

Her eyes widened. "In my town it is not polite for men to speak of a woman's attire," she replied. "Nor to accuse her of being a whore because of it."

"I do apologize," he replied evenly. "I have had a trying day, and I should not have allowed my manners to desert me. Do sit down."

Helga moved to the chair in front of the desk and sat on the edge of the seat. "I do admit that I am somewhat overwhelmed by your city and all of its modern implements," she said. "We do not have such things in my town."

"Are you Amish or something?" Bates asked.

"We are Wulffolk," she replied. "I do not know of the Amish."

Bates turned to Kendall and raised his eyebrows impatiently. "And why have you brought Miss Dordrecht to see me on this incredibly busy day?"

"When I explained to Miss Dordrecht who we were, she told me that she has information about Chief Norwalk that you would find interesting," Kendall said, sitting on the chair next to Helga. He turned to her. "Perhaps you would be willing to share that information with Mayor Bates."

Helga leaned forward and placed her hands on the desk. "I wish to know how I will be compensated for my information," she said.

"It all depends on how important your information turns out to be," Bates replied impatiently.

She shook her head. "My father taught me that good bargaining never happens once you have given the good away," she said. "I require compensation before I share my information."

"This is nonsense," Bates said, and he glared at Kendall. "Did she share the information with you?"

Kendall shook his head. "No, she just told me that she would share Norwalk's secrets," he explained. "But I do think you should listen to her. She has…interesting capabilities."

"What can she do that's so impressive?" Bates asked.

Helga growled deep in her throat, and her face began to transform slowly into that of a wolf. Bates sat back in his chair and watched, his fingers impatiently drumming on the desktop. "So, she can shapeshift," he said to Kendall. "I have a half dozen witches who can do the same. Even that idiot Buck could shapeshift into a wolf. I'm not impressed here."

Helga resumed her human form and shook her head. "I do not frighten you?" she asked.

Bates shrugged. "I've seen better," he replied. "But I'll tell you what. If your information about Norwalk is good, I will bring you into my organization." He reached across the table and covered her hand with his. "I believe that you and I would get along very well."

She pulled her hand away quickly. "You mistake things, Mayor Bates," she said. "I am a woman untouched, and I do not dally with men."

"You're a virgin?" Bates asked, astonished.

"We do not use such terms," Helga replied, insulted. "I am a modest, chaste mistress."

Bates sat back in his chair and studied the woman, stroking his chin slowly. "Well, well," he said. "It seems that once again I owe you an apology. And I honor you for your chastity." He smiled broadly. "I now understand completely who I am dealing with, and I have been looking for someone like you to be part of this organization. I have a crucial role I'd like you to play—a role that holds great honor and esteem, fitting for a woman just like you."

"And you would give me this position if I tell you Joseph's secrets?" she asked, an eager smile on her face.

"Oh, yes. I give you my word that I will give you this position and all the glory and benefits that comes with it," he said.

"Very well," she said with a smile, holding out her hand to him. "It is a deal."

The mayor reached over and clasped her hand in his own. "Yes, it is a deal," he repeated. "Now tell me what I need to know about Norwalk."

"Joseph Norwalk will not be your problem for very much longer," she said with a satisfied smile.

"And why is that?" Mayor Bates asked.

"Because by the next full moon he will be dead."

Chapter Forty-one

"So, are we going to talk?" Hazel asked Joseph later that day as she rounded up the first doe and led it to the milking stand.

"There's really nothing to talk about," Joseph replied distantly.

"Okay, now that's magic," she said as she moved the electric milkers onto the goat's teats. "I had no idea you could do that."

"What?" he asked suspiciously, folding his arms over his chest.

"Be a human, a wolf and an ass all at the same time," she replied.

He bit back the smile, but not before she saw it. With her hand on the goat's withers, she turned to him. "Talk to me," she coaxed. "I can tell that something is bothering you."

He shook his head. "I need to get going," he said, turning and walking toward the door. "Helga is out there somewhere, and I need to round her up."

The door slammed shut in front of him before he could leave. He stood silently for a moment, just looking at the door that Hazel had slammed shut, then slowly turned around. "If you're going to be childish..." he began.

He saw the flash of anger in her eyes, then the hurt. He really regretted the hurt.

"Childish?" she asked. "Oh, I can do childish."

She waved her hand, and a bucket of water levitated and slowly made its way towards Joseph. He just watched it come and waited, thinking he deserved it and more.

"You know," Hazel said, holding back tears, "it's not worth it. Go find Helga. Go do your important things while I stay here living my childish life."

"Hazel," he said regretfully, stepping towards her.

She shook her head. "No, don't bother," she replied, her voice even. "I don't know what's bothering you, but I'm willing to listen and help if I can. That's all I'm going to say."

"It's not your burden," he said simply. Then he opened the door and walked out.

"But we could have shared it," she whispered through tears. She took a deep breath and laid her head on the goat's flank. "Why do men have to be so difficult?"

"I think it has something to do with our hormone levels," Henry said from the doorway. "Do you want company?"

Hazel lifted her head and nodded, her eyes filling with tears. "Sure," she said. "Thanks."

"So, he didn't tell you anything?" he asked, coming alongside her.

She shook her head and wiped away a few stray tears. "It's not my burden," she said sarcastically.

"Ah, the strong, self-sacrificing type," Henry replied.

A quirk of a smile appeared on Hazel's lips. "Is that an anthropological term?" she asked.

He smiled at her. "Well, not officially," he said. "But it should be."

"So, um, professor, how does one deal with the strong, self-sacrificing type?" she asked.

"I haven't a clue," he said. "I'm the bumbling, hesitant, egghead type myself."

She chuckled softly and then sighed sadly. "I think I could love him, Henry," she admitted.

"Yeah, it kind of looked that way," he said, then smiled when she looked up at him with surprise on her face. "Speaking only in a purely academic way."

"Okay, so only in a purely academic way, what am I supposed to do?" she asked.

Henry put his arm around Hazel and hugged her. "There's not a whole lot you can do but wait until he's ready to share his secrets," Henry said.

"That's not what I wanted to hear," she replied.

"I know," he said. "But it's the truth. It sucks, but it's the truth."

She sighed loudly. "Why does this whole moving towards a relationship have to be so difficult?" she moaned.

"Because there are people involved," Henry said. "And whenever there are people involved, things are difficult."

She nodded. "You've got that right."

The goat bleated.

"Oh, it looks like Henrietta's finished," Hazel said, extracting herself from Henry's hug and turning to the goat. She unhooked Henrietta from the milking machine and then led her off the milking stand.

"Okay, Florence," she called. "You're up."

A tall, dove-colored Nubian came forward and rubbed her head against Hazel's side. "Yes, I love you too, Florence," Hazel said, leaning down and pressing her face against the goat's face. "Ready for some treats?"

She led Florence up onto the milking stand, scooped some grain into the feeder, and then fastened her in before attaching the milkers.

Then she turned back to Henry. "So, where were we?"

He smiled and shook his head. "You are amazing with them, you know," he said.

"Mutual admiration," she replied. "Now why did you come over here in the first place? Certainly not to hear my whining."

"You weren't whining. You were sad, and you had a perfect right to be sad," Henry said. "But, I did come for a purpose. Rowan and I are trying to figure out the mystery of the missing men. I was wondering if you might have some extra Joseph DNA laying around."

"Are you asking me if I had him pee in a cup?" she asked.

He chuckled and shook his head. "No, a strand of hair would do."

"As a matter of fact, I do. He left his clothing from the other night in the barn," she said. "I put it away so no one would see it. I'd bet it's got his DNA all over it."

"That's great," he said. Then he ran his hand through his hair. "But she still hasn't explained to me how we are going to test his DNA."

Hazel shook her head. "You think that with Rowan's PhD in Biochemistry she hasn't figured out how to use her abilities to break down DNA yet?"

Henry shook his head in amazement. "Are you kidding me?"

Hazel grinned. "Yes. Yes, I am," she said. "She picked up a used DNA analyzer a year ago when she was doing some work with hybrids."

"Have I mentioned how much I love and admire your sister?" he said fondly.

"You kind of act that way," Hazel teased. "Speaking only in a purely academic way."

Henry laughed and nodded. "Okay, I'll take his stuff and find some samples. We got a sample from Gabriella before we left her room, and we want to compare them."

"You two are like mad scientists together," she replied. "I can't wait to see what you find out."

Chapter Forty-two

Hazel sat in an overstuffed recliner, a box of cookies in her lap and a glass of milk on the end table next to her. The television was on, and a romantic movie was playing on the screen. With a shake of her head, she lifted the remote and pressed a button. Suddenly, a horror flick was playing.

Agnes looked up from where she was sitting at the table working on her lap-top. "Hazel, sweetheart," she inquired. "What are you doing?"

Hazel picked up another cookie and took a bite. "I'm watching TV," she said disconsolately.

Agnes pushed her laptop back on the table, slipped out of her chair and walked over to stand behind Hazel's chair. "What kind of program?" she asked.

Hazel sighed. "The story of my life," she said.

"Is that the name of the movie?" Agnes asked.

Hazel chuckled and shook her head. "No, I have a chick flick on one channel," she said, lifting up the remote and demonstrating. "And every time the couple gets close to kissing, I change it to this horror flick where everyone is screaming and running away from each other. Because that, mommy dear, is the story of my life."

"Well, it's a good thing you're not being overly dramatic or anything," Agnes teased.

Hazel stuck her tongue out at her mother in response.

Agnes leaned forward to gaze at the television. "Is it a werewolf movie?" she asked.

Hazel gasped and looked up at her mother. "Wait! How did you know?" she asked. "Did Rowan tell you?"

Agnes came around the chair, pulled up a brightly-colored hassock and sat down in front of her daughter. "No, Rowan didn't tell me," she said. "My mother told me."

"She came back as a ghost?" Hazel asked, clicking off the television and giving her whole attention to her mother.

278

Agnes picked up a cookie from the box and took a bite. "No, she told me when she was still alive," she said. "But she made me promise to keep it a secret."

"So, why spill the beans now?" Hazel replied.

"Because you went to help Joseph in the village," she said. "And you've been conspicuous about avoiding telling me anything about it."

"He made us promise," Hazel said.

Agnes smiled. "Same goes," she said with a laugh.

Hazel smiled for a moment, then shook her head sadly. "And that was three days ago," she said. "And we haven't heard anything from Joseph since."

Agnes's eyes softened in sympathy. "Three days?" she asked. "Oh sweetheart, I'm so sorry."

Hazel shrugged. "I always fall in love too easily," she said. "I'll get over it. I always do."

Agnes reached out and stroked her daughter's hair. "But this was a little different than usual, wasn't it?"

Tears welled up in Hazel's eyes, and she nodded slowly. "It was always a game before," she whispered. "Like being part of a chick flick. I'd flirt and tease, and they'd do the same. Then we'd go our separate ways but stay friends. No harm, no foul."

"But none of them touched your heart," Agnes said.

Hazel sighed. "None of them hurt like this," she admitted. "And none of them confused me like this. Suddenly, he's gone. Suddenly, he's too busy."

"Well, maybe he is," Agnes said. "Too busy."

"I guess that could be true," Hazel acknowledged with a nod. "But, you know, texting can be done in a second."

"Maybe he doesn't know what to say," Agnes said.

"Why are you on his side?" Hazel asked, leaning forward and placing her head on her mother's shoulder.

Agnes patted her daughter's back and sighed. "I'm on your side," she said. "I'm just trying to help you see all of the possibilities."

"The main possibility is that I was an idiot and saw something that wasn't there," Hazel said sadly. "And now Joseph is embarrassed for me."

"The look I saw on that man's face when he carried you to the house after the explosion had nothing to do with embarrassment," Agnes said. "Why don't you text him?"

"It's his turn," Hazel complained.

Agnes laughed. "But you're the one sitting here, wondering."

"What should I say?"

"Why don't you ask about the child you helped?" Agnes said. "Then you're just being concerned."

"And not desperate," Hazel said excitedly. "Mom, you're brilliant."

Agnes placed a kiss on Hazel's forehead. "I try, my dear. I really try."

281

Chapter Forty-three

"How is Gabriella doing?"

Joseph stared down at his phone for a long time, tapping the side with his thumb. It was a simple question. It was very direct and clear. She wasn't asking about him. She was asking about the child she'd helped.

He wanted her to ask about him.

He placed his phone on his desk and pushed it to the side. He couldn't think about Hazel right now. He had other, more urgent, things to concentrate on. After three days of searching, he'd been unable to locate Helga. He knew that in her wolf state, she could easily travel thirty miles away from the village, but she should have left some tracks somewhere. And he hadn't been able to find anything at all.

He unconsciously reached for the phone again, looked at the message and sighed. He typed, *"She's doing much better. Thank you."*

He stared at his response. Even to him it sounded formal and distant. She didn't deserve that. She had done nothing wrong. He continued to type. *"I miss you."*

"No," he mumbled, moving to erase that last sentence, but instead hit the button to send. "Crap!"

But he couldn't unsend the text.

"Same goes." The new text from Hazel appeared on his screen moments later.

He could hear her voice, see her smile, picture the way her eyes would crinkle when she smiled. "Same goes," he said softly.

A knock on his door had him placing the phone, screen side down, on his desk.

"Yes?" he called out.

Donovan peered inside. "Got a minute?" he asked.

Joseph nodded. "Yeah, come in," he said. "Take a seat."

Closing the door behind him, Donovan sat down across from Joseph and took out his phone. He pressed a button, and electronic noises began to play. Then Donovan leaned forward and lowered his voice. "Have you ever checked this room for listening or recording devices?" he asked softly.

Joseph shook his head. "No," he whispered. "Why?"

Donovan quickly shook his head, then pulled out another device from his jacket pocket. "Shut off your phone and your computer," he whispered.

Joseph reached over and signed off his computer and then reached for his phone. He stared at Hazel's response one more time, then powered down the phone. "Off," he whispered.

Donovan stood up and slowly walked around the room, the device in his hand making soft, intermittent sounds as he moved. Then the sounds began to get louder and closer together. Finally, as he moved to a picture of City Hall on the wall just behind Joseph's desk, the sound peaked and became one long blast. Donovan turned off the device and studied the picture. Then he smiled and nodded. "And we have a winner," he said, lifting the picture frame off the wall.

The small camera was attached to the back of the picture, and ironically, the small lens hole was located where the mayor's office window was situated in the picture.

A small wire was connected to the camera and was fed through a small hole in the wall.

"Audio and video," Joseph said quietly, coming over to the other side of the picture. "I had no idea."

"Yeah, well most police chiefs don't have to worry about being watched," Donovan whispered. "But in this town, if you're not part of the coven, you're a suspect."

Joseph turned to Donovan and leaned against the wall. "So, are you my friend who's come here to show me that I'm being set up?" he whispered. "Or is this whole thing a ploy of yours to get me to trust you?"

Donovan smiled. "Good question," he said. "And you wouldn't believe me if I said that I'm on your side."

286

"No, but I'd believe you if you told me that this was a ploy to gain my confidence," Joseph said, returning the smile. "You want to confess?"

Chuckling softly, Donovan put the picture back on the wall. "You might want to remodel your office," he suggested. "And perhaps move the credenza with the stereo equipment right under this picture."

Joseph nodded. "I tend to play really bad opera music when I'm not in the office," he said. "Really bad."

"Good choice," Donovan replied, turning up the white noise on his phone and placing it on the thick bottom of the frame. "I want to show you something through your window."

They walked across the room to the window, which was out of the range of the camera.

"What's up?" Joseph asked.

"The coven is planning a big ceremony for the Master," Donovan said. "We still have a few months until the curse comes due, but this ceremony is supposed to strengthen the members of the coven."

"Where are they holding it?" Joseph asked.

Donovan shook his head. "They aren't trusting me with the location yet," he said. "But I'm guessing it will be someplace rural— either a forested area or in Kettle Moraine on the bluffs."

"Do you know when?" Joseph asked.

"Yeah, the next full moon," Donovan said. "Which coincidentally is a lunar eclipse, so it's going to be…"

"A blood moon," Joseph finished. "Yes, I know. And it's next Thursday night."

"So, if you could make sure the Willoughbys are covered…" Donovan began.

"I can't make that promise," Joseph said.

"What the hell?" Donovan asked. "There's nothing more important than making sure they're protected, especially if the entire coven is gathered near their neck of the woods."

Joseph nodded. "I agree," he said. "You need to tell them about it."

288

"I can't," Donovan said. "I'm risking enough talking to you. They have me watched wherever I go, and even my electronic communication is bugged. I will only cause them further problems if I try and contact them."

"Okay, I'll let them know," Joseph agreed. "But I can't promise to be there with them. I will if I can…"

Donovan studied him for a moment. "You're not running scared, are you?" he asked.

"No, I'm not," Joseph replied angrily. Then he sighed and shook his head. "But I guess I can understand why you might think that. No, I will protect them if I can, but things might be beyond my control. I'll do my best."

"Can I help with this out of your control thing?" Donovan asked.

Joseph shook his head. "No. No one can help."

Chapter Forty-four

Cat drove the Jeep down Main Street and parked across the street from the police station. Everything had been quiet at the house, and with the store closed, she needed to get out or she would go crazy. Joseph had come by the store earlier that week, had taken photos of the outside and had bagged some evidence near the front entrance. Following up on the photos and evidence was her excuse for driving into town.

She put the Jeep into park and reached for the door handle when she saw Donovan walking out of the station. Moving the seat back so the body of the Jeep hid her from view, she watched through her side mirror as Donovan quickly jogged across the parking lot and moved toward his car.

Her heart pounded, and while part of her prayed that he wouldn't glance over and notice her, another part hoped that he would. Her pulse increased, and the palms of her hands grew sweaty as she watched him moving closer to his car. But he didn't falter in his steps or even pause for a moment, but hurried to his car, sliding into the driver's seat without a pause. In a moment, he had started his car and was driving away.

"Even if he had noticed me," she mumbled, "he probably wouldn't have come over. He made it clear the other night that he isn't interested in what we think of him."

She absently rubbed her hand over her heart. It still hurt. She had so wanted him to say that it had all been a lie, that he'd been on their side from the very beginning. She wanted him to ask for her forgiveness and tell her that he'd sacrificed to save her family. She wanted it to be real.

"There is no such thing as happily-ever-after and fairytales," she muttered.

"That's a fairly cynical thing to say."

She gasped and turned to see Donovan standing next to the Jeep with the passenger side door open. "How did you?" she asked.

He slid in and closed the door behind himself. "I made a U-turn and pulled up behind you," he said.

"I didn't think you even saw me," she replied.

He met her eyes, and she shivered at the intensity. "Cat, I don't need to see you," he said softly. "I can feel your presence."

She looked away from him and stared out the windshield. "Get out," she ordered.

"What?" he asked, surprised.

"I said get out," she repeated. Then she turned back to him, her eyes smoldering with anger.

"What did I do?" he asked.

She rolled her eyes. "Oh, Cat," she mocked. "I don't need to see you. I can feel your presence." She stared at him for a long moment. "Do you really think I'm stupid or desperate enough to fall for that line?"

"It's not a line," he said.

"Oh, give me a break," she retorted. "I'm sure you've used it on other women hundreds of times."

He reached over and grabbed her arm. "There have been no other women," he said. "There has only been you."

She placed her hand over his. "Fine, prove it," she said. "Let me read your thoughts."

He immediately pulled his hand away. "I can't, Cat," he said.

"Why Donovan?" she asked. "Afraid I'd find a catalogue of other women who've heard that line?"

He shook his head. "No, you have to believe me," he began.

"No. No, I don't," she said. "I don't have to believe you. And, quite honestly, I can't afford to believe you, because believing you puts my family at risk."

He leaned forward. "I saved you," he said. "I heard about the explosion, and I saved you."

"And maybe that was your plan all along," she replied. "To come out looking like our rescuer so we would welcome you back with open arms, and you would plan our demise."

"How can you believe that of me?" he asked. "We used to love each other."

"Used to, being the important phrase here," Cat replied. "You left. You walked away. And you joined them. You got your power and you got your money." Her voice softened, and she sighed. "I really do hope those things made you happy, Donovan. But, please, go away."

He started to speak, then looked at the pain in her eyes and nodded. "I'll go," he said. "But don't give up on me, Cat."

"Have a nice life, Donovan," she replied. Once he was out, she turned the Jeep on and pulled down the road. Her conversation with Joseph could wait for another day. She wiped a tear off her cheek and took a deep breath. All she wanted to do was go home and cry.

Chapter Forty-five

"Okay, I'm in the library," Hazel said as she sat in the middle of the couch with her eyes closed. Henry was seated on one side of her, holding one hand, and Rowan was seated on the other side, holding her other hand. Then Rowan and Henry held hands, forming a complete circle.

"What am I looking for again?" Hazel asked.

"Something that has to do with Rumspringa," Henry said. "Or anything close to that. It could be Rumspringen or Rumschpringe or even Herumspringen."

Hazel nodded and concentrated on her remote viewing of the shelves in Henrich's library. She quickly skimmed the spines of the books but didn't find anything close to what Henry had been looking for. "Okay, there are no titles with that word in it," she reported.

Henry shook his head. "Yeah, I don't think there would be titles," he agreed. "But there may be some information about it in some old journals."

Hazel nodded. "Okay, so if they don't use that word in particular, I'm just looking for some kind of rite of passage, right?"

"Exactly," Rowan said. "In Amish and Mennonite communities, there is a rite of passage for adolescent boys called Rumspringa. They often leave their villages and see what the world outside is like."

"So, you're thinking the Wulffolk men are doing something similar," Hazel said. "And that's where they lose them?"

"Either that or their rite of passage includes kicking the young men out of the town to find another place to live," Henry added.

Hazel paused in her perusal of the books. "Why would they do that?" she asked. "Why would they kick them out?"

"Well, in wolf packs, when adolescent males reach maturity, they leave their home territory to search for a mate. This leaves the alpha male free to produce the litters in his pack," Henry replied.

"Wait," Hazel said. "Henrich is the alpha male in the pack? Then all the women in the village... Can I just say ew?"

"I'm not saying that's what's happening," Henry inserted. "But, that's one plausible explanation for the lack of men."

"I'm sticking with ew," Hazel said, and then she paused for a moment. "Oh, hey, here we go. An old journal that looks like it dates back to the eighties."

"1880s?" Henry asked.

"No, 1980s," Hazel replied. "Isn't that old enough?"

Henry nodded.

"Henry, I can't hear you nod," Hazel said, her eyes still closed.

"Oh, sorry," he replied, shrugging when Rowan chuckled. "Guess I need to get more used to this remote viewing practice."

Hazel smiled. "It was great when Cat was on a date," she said. "I could give everyone minute by minute reports."

"I heard that," Cat said as she walked in from the kitchen.

"Damn, why didn't anyone warn me?" Hazel said with a smile.

"She snuck up on all of us," Rowan replied. "So, are you going to send the book?"

She nodded. "Yep, incoming," she called, and a book fell out of the air onto the coffee table in front of them. "How'd I do?"

"Perfect aim," Henry replied. "Do you see anything else?"

Hazel started to look around again and then heard the library's doorknob jiggle. "Hey, someone's coming in," she said. "So, I'm coming home."

Henry and Rowan held onto Hazel's hands until she took a deep breath and opened her eyes. Then they let go of her hands. "I'm back," she teased. She rolled her shoulders and stretched her neck. "Sitting there like that takes a lot out of you."

"So, why did you leave when someone was coming in?" Henry asked. "They couldn't see you."

"No, but when someone is intuitive or has any psychic abilities, they can sense me," Hazel said. "And since Joseph said that his grandfather had some of Merlin's blood, I didn't want to take the chance."

Rowan reached over and picked up the book. "I don't think Henrich would mind us borrowing this journal," she said.

"Unless they murder all the men after the age of sixteen in some weird ceremony," Hazel countered. "Then, yeah, he'd probably mind."

"Okay, if Henrich could sense you, then how did you get away with spying on Cat?" Henry asked.

Hazel grinned at her oldest sister. "Well, generally, her abilities were fairly muddled by the time I'd check on her," she teased. "And the car windows were pretty steamed up too."

"I'm going to get some work done," Cat said quietly, quickly leaving the room. "Good luck with your research."

"I've stepped in it again," Hazel said, standing up and moving around Rowan. "I'm going to go talk to her. You two check out the journal. Okay?"

She started to walk away when Rowan reached over and grabbed her hand. "You didn't mean to hurt her," she said. "It was good-natured fun."

Hazel nodded. "Yeah, I know," she said. "Thanks."

Chapter Forty-six

The small office was tucked away in a cozy corner on the south side of the house. A little hallway in front of the office door offered access to a cute half-bath and a door that led to a small parking area for those who came to meet with one of the Willoughbys. Vintage floral prints were displayed on the walls, and a large bouquet of dried lavender sat in a tall, copper urn next to the door. Hazel balanced the tray she was carrying on her hip to free up her hand to knock on the office door.

"Come in," Cat called from inside.

Hazel turned the knob, pushed the door open, readjusted the tray in her hands and then entered the room. She pushed the door closed again with her foot and walked over to the large table in the center of the room. Cat was seated at a counter along one wall, her eyes glued to the display before her.

Hazel set the tray in the center of the table and waited for Cat to turn away from the keyboard. "Just a second," Cat said slowly, concentrating on the screen in front of her.

"Take your time," Hazel said, sliding into one of the upholstered chairs that surrounded the table. She picked up the teapot on the tray and poured herself a cup of tea. Its fragrance filled the room.

"Not fair," Cat complained as she continued to type. "That smells really good."

"I'll pour you a cup," Hazel offered. "Two sugars, right?"

"That would be great," Cat replied.

Hazel poured the tea, added the sugars and then walked around the table to Cat's side. She looked down onto the screen and shook her head in confusion. "Why are they cancelling their order?" she asked, looking at the online correspondence from one of their loyal customers.

Cat sat back in her chair. "Well, it seems that somehow the shipment of lavender and calendula face lotion had fecal matter in it," she said tightly.

"Well, it's organic," Hazel replied. "I mean, everyone knows that you can expect up to one percent of fecal matter. It's only goat poop. It's not going to hurt you."

Cat looked up at Hazel. "This was more like 99 percent fecal matter," she said. "And it smelled more like swine poop than goat poop."

"How did that…" Hazel began and then stopped. "Wanda!"

"Or someone from the coven," Cat said. "If they can't destroy the store, they will destroy our business."

Hazel turned and perched on the end of the counter. "So, how many boxes did the customer open?" she asked.

"Just one," Cat replied. "And they opened six jars in a 24-pack case."

"So, where is their warehouse?" Hazel asked.

"What are you thinking?" Cat asked.

"Well, the only rule is an harm it none, right?" Hazel asked. "So, there's no harm in putting back what we originally put in. I could just transform the poop into the lotion in the rest of the boxes. And, I can also change the labeling on the outside of the opened box to read something like lab samples. Then we can apologize that shipping sent them the wrong thing."

"You have a dangerous and creative mind," Cat said with a smile. Then she nodded. "Okay, do it."

Hazel looked at the shipping address on the invoice and then closed her eyes.

What we shipped to beautify

Was altered to become swine pie.

Reverse the spell with all due speed.

As I ask, so mote it be.

"Swine pie?" Cat asked.

"You know, like cow pie," Hazel replied.

"Yes, I know," Cat said, shaking her head. "But swine pie?"

Hazel grinned. "I'm a witch, not a poet," she said.

"Give me a second," Cat said, taking a sip of the tea. "I just need to call the customer and tell her about the mix-up."

"Yeah, lay on some of that Catalpa Willoughby charm and sophistication," Hazel said.

In a few minutes, the customer was not only delighted but also laughing about the mix-up.

"Once again, I apologize," Cat said. "Thank you so much for your understanding. And let me take five percent off your invoice for your trouble. No, that's fine. Have a great day."

She hung up the phone and picked up the teacup. "Now, this is just what I need," she said, then took another sip.

"I brought cookies," Hazel said.

Cat's eyes widened in delight when Hazel lifted the cover from the platter filled with an assortment of cookies. "What's going on?" Cat asked. "It's not my birthday."

Hazel went over and hugged her sister. "No, it's my way of saying I'm sorry for hurting your feelings."

Cat hugged Hazel back. "Oh, honey, you didn't hurt my feelings," she said. "You were just teasing. I was just a little tender just then."

"Donovan?" Hazel asked, levitating the plate so it hovered right next to them.

Cat picked up a cookie and bit down with a snap. "Yes," she said. "I saw him in town."

"Men suck," Hazel said, biting into her own cookie.

Cat nodded. "Yes, they do," she agreed.

"I sent Joseph a text this afternoon," Hazel admitted, and when Cat looked aghast, she shook her head. "I only asked about Gabriella. Mom's idea."

"Okay, that was brilliant," Cat said, finishing off her cookie and reaching for another.

"That's what I thought too," she replied. "Then he texted back, telling me that Gabriella was doing better,

306

thanking me for asking, and then he said that he missed me."

"He actually texted that?" Cat asked. "So, what did you do?"

"I texted, 'same goes,'" she replied.

"And then?"

"And then nothing," Hazel said. "Nothing at all." She picked up another cookie. "Men suck. What did Donovan do?"

"He snuck into my car and told me that he could sense my presence without even seeing me," she said.

"What, like a dog?" Hazel asked.

Cat spewed cookies across the table. "Hey, that's not fair," she choked as she laughed. "Besides, who are you to talk about men and dogs here?"

"Wolf. Joseph's a wolf. Actually, according to Henry, Joseph is a cryptozoological bipedal lycanthrope."

"That's sounds impressive," Cat said with a grin.

"It probably means that he has to turn around three times before he can lie down," Hazel quipped.

"He probably sheds," Cat added.

Hazel handed Cat another cookie. "This one's on me," she said. "See, we don't need men. We have each other."

Hazel's phone alerted her to a text message, and she looked down. "Crap!" she exclaimed.

"What?" Cat asked.

"It's Joseph. He's on his way here to talk to us," she replied, panicked. "How do I look?"

Cat grinned. "Wait, I thought we don't need men," she reminded her sister.

Hazel nodded. "We don't," she agreed. "But I want to make sure he knows what he's missing out on."

Chapter Forty-seven

Hazel jogged into the great room and hurried over to the couch where Rowan and Henry were studying the journal she'd filched from Henrich's library. "Hey, I wanted to let you two know that Joseph is on his way over," she said. "So, you might want to hide that journal. I'm going to run upstairs and change into something..."

"Hazel," Rowan said, looking up at her sister with her face filled with concern.

"What?" Hazel asked, immediately sitting down on the coffee table in front of them.

"It's about Joseph," Henry said with a sigh. "Actually, it's about all of the men from Wulffolk."

"What?" Hazel repeated.

"We were right about Rumspringa," Rowan said, and then she shook her head. "Well, not entirely right. But they do have a rite of passage when the men are in their teens and twenties."

"Okay, so they go get drunk," Hazel said, feeling a pit growing in her stomach. "No big deal, right?"

"No, it *is* a big deal," Henry said. "And it has nothing to do with getting drunk or running around without rules. When the men of Wulffolk reach a certain age, they turn into wolves, and they don't turn back."

"How? How could that happen?" she exclaimed.

"It probably has something to do with intermarriage," Rowan supplied. "Often when a small community keeps intermarrying within itself for generations, the less desirable genetic traits become dominant."

"And turning into a wolf and staying there would be one of those less desirable traits?" Hazel asked slowly.

"One of them," Henry said.

"There's something else?" Hazel asked.

"Hazel," Rowan said, reaching out and holding her sister's hands. "From what the journal says, there are three options. One is they turn into a wolf. The second is that they remain in the werewolf kind of state and can't change back to human form."

Rowan glanced at Henry, and he nodded sadly.

"What?" Hazel demanded. "What is the third option?"

"Sometimes the final change is too much for their bodies," Henry said. "And they don't make it."

"They die?" Hazel whispered hoarsely, her eyes filling with tears. She shook her head, the room turning into a blur. "No. That can't be right. Maybe the journal writer is wrong."

"The journal was written by a wise woman," Henry said. "She took care of the young men. She was with them until whatever happened occurred."

"But why aren't the wolf people in the village?" Hazel asked. "Do they hide?"

"They leave," Rowan explained. "They leave because they forget. They forget who they were. They forget their families. They become beasts of the woods."

311

"But this isn't going to happen to Joseph, right?" she said. "This can't happen to him because he's older than that." She wiped the tears from her face. "And he told me that his mother was Native American, so that whole recessive gene thing doesn't apply."

"There were others who were only half Wulffolk that she studied," Rowan said slowly. "Hon, it didn't stop things. It only slowed things down. They were changed or…or gone by the time they turned thirty."

Hazel took a deep breath and nodded her head. "Okay, well, they didn't have a PhD in biochemistry or a professor like Henry or the power of the Willoughby family," she said. "So, we'll just have to find a cure. That's all."

"You're right," Henry said. "That's what we need to do. But we have a small complication."

"What?" Hazel asked.

"These changes occur at a full moon," Rowan said. "And the journal had a record of Joseph's birth. He turns thirty at the next full moon."

Hazel jumped up and walked away from them. "No. No, you have to be wrong," she said. "What about Henrich or the other older men in the village? Well, what about them?"

"The genetic trait didn't start appearing until the seventies and eighties, so boys born in the early sixties were the first ones to exhibit the problem. Henrich was probably born in the forties or fifties."

"There has to be a way," she said, turning to Henry and Rowan. "There just has to be a way."

Chapter Forty-eight

A knock on the back door startled Agnes from her reading. Unaware of what was happening in the other part of the house, she casually took off her reading glasses, placed them next her teacup on the small table next to her chair, and stood up to answer the door.

"Oh, Joseph," she said with a delighted smile once she opened the door. "It's so nice to see you again. Are you here to visit?"

Joseph, dressed in his uniform, shook his head. "I'm sorry, no," he said, keeping his tone professional. "I texted Hazel that I need to speak with all of you about some information I discovered this afternoon."

"Oh," Agnes replied, her smile leaving her face. She stepped back and opened the door wider. "Well, come in, please. I think the rest of the family is in the great room."

Joseph stepped into the kitchen. "Thank you, Agnes," he said. "This won't take too long."

314

"Well, you go on in," Agnes said, motioning in the direction of the great room. "I need to get my glasses and my tea. I'm sure they're expecting you."

Joseph walked down the hallway between the kitchen and the great room and stopped at the entrance, his focus on Hazel pacing across the room. He could see that she was visibly upset. He started to speak when Hazel turned back to Rowan and Henry, who were sitting on the couch.

"There has to be a way," she cried. "There just has to be a way."

The fear and agony in her voice spurned him to action. "A way to do what?" he asked, stepping into the room.

Hazel turned quickly and stared at him in astonishment for a moment. Then she ran across the room at him. "You!" she screamed, pushing her hands against his chest with all her might but not making any impact on him at all.

Her anger was seething. She stepped back and then flew at him again. "How dare you!" she exclaimed, pushing at him again. But once again, he stood his ground.

"Would you like me to step back?" he teased.

She lifted her eyes to his, and he was struck by the pain in them. She put her hand over her mouth to muffle a sob, then shook her head. "You can do whatever you damn well want to do," she whispered. "I'm leaving."

She ran around him, through the kitchen and out the back door.

He didn't hesitate for a moment. He turned around and ran after her.

"Hazel," he called, running down the patio steps after her. "Wait."

He watched as she waved her hand behind her, and suddenly his parked patrol car rolled in front of him. He skirted around the car and continued to follow her to the barn. She stopped at the barn door, glanced over her shoulder, waved her hand again, and the tractor from inside the barn rolled out to block his access to the door.

316

He jumped up into the seat of the tractor and jumped down the other side, pushing the door open before she had the chance to lock it. "We need to talk," he said.

She walked across the barn, her face away from him. Reaching the other side of the barn, she gripped a wooden post near the stalls as if her life depended on it. "Go away," she said, stifling a sob. "Remember, it's your burden."

He strode over to her, put his hands on her shoulders, and began to turn her around. "What are you talking…" he stopped when he looked down at her red-rimmed eyes, her face awash with tears, and her body trembling in reaction.

"Hazel," he whispered, wiping her tears with his thumb. "What happened?"

"What happened?" she asked, pushing him away and wiping her cheeks with her arm. "What happened? You lied to me."

He shook his head. "I didn't lie to you," he exclaimed.

"You didn't tell me," she threw back. "That's a lie. Not telling is a lie."

Confused about the subject of their argument, Joseph felt he still had to defend his honor. "No, not telling is not telling," he argued. "There are some things that need to be confidential."

She kicked an empty metal bucket at her feet and sent it spinning across the floor. "That's crap," she said. "It's all about whether or not you trust someone."

"What does trust have to do with this?" he asked, putting his hands on her shoulders again. "What the hell are we talking about anyway?"

She inhaled sharply, her breath shuddering, and she looked up at him. "I don't want you to die," she whispered.

A punch to his solar plexus could not have taken the air out of him as quickly as her whispered statement and the look in her eyes. She cared if he lived or died. She simply cared.

318

He bent down and brushed his mouth over her lips. "Hazel," he breathed.

She wrapped her arms around his neck and clung to him, crying, "Oh, Joseph, you can't die," she wept. "I couldn't...I couldn't bear it."

He kissed her again, tasting the salt from her tears on his lips, and then he pulled her into his arms and held her. "Shhhhh," he whispered against her hair. "It will be fine."

"How can it be fine if you only have a week to live?" she stammered against his chest.

"What did you say to Rowan and Henry?" he asked gently, kissing her forehead. "There has to be a way."

She looked up at him and shook her head. "Why?" she asked. "Why do you believe that now?"

He looked deeply into her eyes and smiled sadly. "Because now I have a reason to live," he replied, and he pulled her into his arms once again.

Chapter Forty-nine

Cat nibbled on one more cookie as she sat in the office finishing up her work. She smiled as she looked at the half empty tea cup and remembered Hazel's quick departure from the room when she received the text from Joseph.

"Sure, Hazel. Men suck," she chuckled softly. "And you totally have no feelings for Joseph."

Suddenly, Cat's vision started to blur, and the room began to fade away before her. Knowing this was the onset of a vision, she put the cookie on her desk, leaned back in her chair and closed her eyes.

At first Cat saw nothing but darkness. Then the scene before her began to fill with light. She felt like she was walking from a distance toward a clearing in the woods. She looked and saw Henry and Rowan standing together hand in hand. They weren't speaking to each other, but she could feel they were helping each other, working together.

Her mother was a few feet away, and she seemed to be searching for something. She was walking around the clearing and calling out, but Cat couldn't hear what she was saying.

Then she saw Hazel kneeling on the ground. Her head was bent forward, her face hidden behind her long hair. Finally, Hazel lifted her head, and Cat could see tracks of tears on her face. Her expression showed intense sorrow and grief. Then her expression lightened, and she stood up and walked to the end of the clearing, her arms open in welcome. Cat strained to recognize the figure walking from the woods toward Hazel.

Finally, she saw him. Joseph, as a wolfman, was walking towards Hazel. As he stepped into the clearing, he took Hazel's hands in his own and bent his head to kiss her. She moved into his embrace, and then suddenly the two of them seemed to merge into each other, creating one being for a few moments. Then they separated, and Joseph was a man.

The vision darkened, and, after a moment, Cat opened her eyes. She took a deep cleansing breath and picked up the cookie for one more bite. "It would seem," she said to herself, "that Joseph is a part of this whole thing."

She pushed herself out of her chair and walked toward the door. It was time to move to the next step.

Agnes peered out the kitchen window and watched Hazel and Joseph walk back to the house arm in arm. "Well, I guess they cleared that up," she said.

"What?" Rowan asked, scooting in to stand next to her mother and seeing the two together. "Okay, well maybe we'll get him to cooperate now."

"Cooperate?" Agnes asked. "Are you talking about the Rumspringa?"

"You know about that?" Henry asked.

She nodded. "My mother told me," Agnes replied. "She had a relationship with the wise woman of the village."

"Joseph turns thirty by the next full moon," Rowan said.

Agnes looked back through the window and saw the love shining from her daughter's face. "We have to cast a circle," Agnes insisted. "We've waited long enough."

"You're right," Cat said as she entered the kitchen. "We do need to cast a circle."

Agnes turned from the window and looked at her daughter. "This is a little sudden, coming from you," she said, surprised.

"I just had a vision, and Joseph played a part," Cat replied. "I don't understand everything I saw, but I agree that Joseph is part of this journey."

Hazel and Joseph entered the kitchen.

"We're going to cast a circle," Agnes told them.

"What?" Joseph asked.

"Don't worry," Henry assured Joseph. "It's an experience that you don't want to miss."

Joseph looked down at Hazel, and she nodded. "I think it's a good idea," she said. "We gain more information when we cast a circle, and we're protected from outside influences."

"Protected?" he asked. "Like no one can see or hear what you're doing?"

Hazel nodded.

Joseph turned to Agnes. "While we're in the circle, may I speak with all of you about the information I received today?"

"Yes, of course," Agnes said. "But let's get started right away."

They moved into the great room, and Hazel waved her hand to move the big table and a large, braided rug. Underneath the rug was a Celtic knot embedded into the wooden floor. The quaternary knot was made up of four ovals that intersected with each other and an outer circle that threaded its way through all of them. The entire circle was about nine feet in diameter. Each of the women stood on one of the outer points of an oval, and Henry directed Joseph to stand in the middle with him.

The air in the room changed, and the women around the circle changed with it. These were women of power with the blood of ancient sorceresses flowing through their veins. Their eyes were alert, and their skin glowed with energy. Their hair seemed to flow around their heads, tossed on waves of their combined energies.

Agnes lifted a smudge stick up high above her head, a wisping, gray trail of smoke in the air behind it, and then drew a straight line down. "I cleanse the space to the east."

Catalpa, standing in the next clockwise space, lifted her smudge stick as her mother had and said, "I cleanse the space to the south."

Hazel, in the next space, also lifted her smudge stick in the same manner. "I cleanse the space to the west," she said softly.

Then Rowan repeated the same actions and said, "I cleanse my space to the north."

When Rowan was done, all the women turned and walked clockwise around the edge of the circle, waving their smudge sticks and chanting, "We cleanse all spaces in between."

Joseph inhaled the acrid scent of white sage, recognizing it from ceremonies he'd witnessed during his stay with his mother's people. "White sage," he whispered to Henry.

Henry nodded. "It cleanses the air of anything evil or dangerous."

"It smells like the air after a lightning storm," Joseph added.

"Magic flows like electricity," he said, "and creates many of the same chemical reactions as lightning does."

The women stopped walking and paused at the places where they started in the circle. Each one raised her arms out, shoulder-height, so the distance between them from fingertip to fingertip measured about a foot.

"We cast this circle, as is our right," Agnes chanted with her eyes closed, "to protect us with thy holy light. Nothing can harm or corrupt our plea. As we ask, so mote it be."

Suddenly, a beam of ultraviolet light appeared above Agnes and then traveled down from the top of her head and through her arms. The light traveled through her to Rowan and Catalpa on either side of her, through them and then finally to Hazel. The light was warm and bright and lit the inside of the circle with a golden glow.

Agnes opened her eyes and smiled at her daughters. "Well done," she said softly. "Now, let's talk."

The women stepped forward into the circle, but the barrier of light stayed on the edges of the knot, bright and glowing.

Chapter Fifty

Agnes sat on an embroidered pillow and directed all of the others to take seats on similarly decorated pillows inside the circle. Then she turned to Joseph. "Why don't we begin with what you came to talk to us about?" she suggested.

He nodded, then took a deep breath and felt the energy from inside the circle infuse his body. "Thank you," he said softly to Agnes. "My mother's people would say this is a sacred place, and I will remember that as I share this information with you."

He turned and looked at Cat. "This afternoon Donovan came to my office," he explained. "He had information he wanted me to share with all of you. He told me that he could not come here himself, because it would compromise the position he has gained in the coven."

"By compromise, does he mean that he would lose stature?" Cat asked, her voice filled with scorn.

"I believe he could lose his life," Joseph replied evenly, meeting Cat's eyes. "I don't know what to believe about him yet. But if he is playing a game with the coven in order to get information to protect your family, it's a dangerous game."

"But if he is acting like our friend in order to gain power in the coven?" she asked.

"It's still a dangerous game," he replied. "Because he has put himself in the position where no one trusts him."

"What did he tell you?" Agnes asked.

"The coven is going to hold a special meeting during the next full moon," he began.

Hazel gasped softly, and Joseph took her hand in his and squeezed it gently.

"What?" Cat asked, watching the interaction between the two of them.

"That conversation is next on the agenda," Agnes replied. "Go on, Joseph."

"Donovan said that it will be a ceremony honoring the Master," he said.

Suddenly the light around the circle shimmered and darkened momentarily. Everyone looked up in surprise, watching as the wall of light deepened to a lavender color and then slowly worked its way back up the light spectrum to golden yellow.

"What just happened?" Joseph asked.

"After we're finished, we need to check the house," Agnes said. "It seems that we have uninvited guests observing us. But the power of the circle protected us."

She turned to Joseph. "It also seems that it is activated by the use of that name you just mentioned," she said. "So, we should avoid using that name."

"We need a code name," Hazel suggested. "How about mosquito, because it's an annoying, blood-sucking pest?"

Cat smiled. "I'm good with that," she said. "And because we are going to slap it down and destroy it."

Rowan grinned. "I like the way you think," she agreed. "Okay, the M-word is now Mosquito."

Joseph nodded. "So, this ceremony, honoring the mosquito, is going to be held on the night of the full moon, which is also a blood moon. He said that it will strengthen the mosquito's power and the power of the members of the coven."

"Did he know where it was going to be held?" Henry asked.

"No, he didn't," Joseph replied, shaking his head. "He said they were keeping that information from him because they didn't trust him. But he thought it would be in a wooded area or perhaps on top of one of the bluffs in Kettle Moraine."

"The full moon is only a week away," Cat said.

Hazel nodded. "Yes, I know," she said. Then she turned to her mother. "We should talk about the next thing on the agenda."

Agnes nodded, then turned to Cat. "Before we do that," she said, "I'm curious about your vision and why you wanted us to cast a circle with Joseph."

"You had a vision with Joseph in it?" Hazel asked.

Cat nodded. "It was after you got his text and left the room," she said. "And it was a little confusing."

She recounted the vision, making sure she included every detail, and then paused, looking around the circle. "Does that make sense to anyone?" she asked.

"Perhaps," Henry offered. "Joseph has a genetic, ticking time bomb in his body, which is scheduled to go off on the same day as the Ma... I mean, mosquito's ceremony."

"The night of the full moon," Cat clarified.

"Yes. From what Rowan and I have discovered," Henry paused and turned to Joseph. "We have made liberal use of your grandfather's library to learn more about your village." Then he turned back to Cat. "Because of the limited number of people in the village, there was quite a bit of inbreeding over the generations. Starting in about the sixties, this caused one particular recessive trait to appear in connection with the Y chromosome."

"So, it affects males," Cat said.

Henry nodded. "Exactly," he said. "Males who have aged past adolescence, generally between the ages of seventeen and thirty."

"We discovered that even those with a parent who was not within the Wulffolk community had a tendency to have this trait, but it displayed its effect in later years," Rowan added.

"What is the effect?" Cat asked.

"Death," Joseph said plainly. "Or I turn into a wolfman or wolf, lose my memory, and wander aimlessly for the rest of my life."

Cat took a deep breath. "That doesn't sound like a much better alternative to death," she said.

He shook his head. "I agree," he said. Then he turned to Rowan. "With your research, have you found anything to correct it?"

"I'd like to get some DNA samples from your grandfather," Rowan said. "And compare them with your samples and see where the change takes place."

"You have my samples?" he asked, turning to look at Hazel.

"You left your clothes in the barn," she replied with a smile.

He nodded. "Thank you," he said. "I'll get the samples from my grandfather. But in the meantime, we need to put together some security measures to protect all of you from the mosquito."

"The only thing that's going to protect us is conquering him once and for all," Cat said. "Which is why I brought Henry's grandmother's grimoire into the circle with us tonight."

Chapter Fifty-one

Cat slid the old, leather-bound book out from beneath her large pillow and placed it in the middle of the circle.

Henry looked down at the book, his ancestor's possession, and then up at Cat. "Are you sure?" he asked. "We've talked about opening it before, and it didn't feel right to you."

She met his eyes and shook her head. "Honestly, Henry, I'm not sure," she admitted. "I am so confused about everything right now. I don't think I can trust myself, and that's why I think we need more direction."

"Okay," he said gently. "I'll give it a try."

He laid his hand on the cover of the book and repeated the phrase that had sprung into his mind the first time he'd seen the old book, "Memores acti prudentes future."

Joseph looked questioningly at the group, and
Rowan nodded. "Mindful of deeds done, aware of things
to come," she whispered.

The book seemed to glow underneath Henry's
hand, the binding turning from old brown to golden
brown. The brass latch on the side of the book sprung
open, and Henry lifted his hand, opened the cover of the
book, and began to read.

"Dear family,

We write these words the evening before we go to
battle against the demon the Pratt Institute members
unwittingly released into our community. We do not use
the term battle lightly, for this creature of darkness is not a
partner or a mentor, as many of our ilk consider it to be.

It is a destroyer.

It would destroy our families and our community
and replace them with solitude and paranoia. It would
destroy our capacity to have charity one for another, and
replace it with hate and prejudice. It would destroy our
gratitude for the blessings we now enjoy and replace that

336

with envy and greed. In fact, it would steal our souls and the very essence that marks humanity with hope and love.

For this cause, for the cause of humanity, love, hope and family, we are willing to lay down our lives and entrap this creature of the dark. But, by making this decision, dear family, we have bound you to this quest. We now realize that the souls of the three (well, truthfully, the four) of us are only powerful enough to trap the beast for one hundred and twenty years. You will need more than the three from one to destroy the beast.

The three must find partners, those of the blood, who love deeply enough to sacrifice themselves for the quest. Without the three (and, perhaps, one more soul) the beast will not be conquered, and humanity will be defeated.

As the time draws nearer, you will find the creature, even within its prison, will have power to influence the hearts and minds of those who were already turned to hate and greed. It can even turn the hearts of those who were once good but thought they could control the power of the creature. That is one of the clever tricks of the beast, and a slippery slope to enslavement by its powers.

We ask you now, our dear family, to find those partners and then return to this grimoire within the safety of a circle to read more of your task.

Blessed be our sisters and our daughters."

Henry carefully closed the book, and the latch sprang back into place. He sat back and took a deep breath. "I could feel their fear for you," he said. "As I read their words, it was like they were reaching out from the grave with their warnings."

"What did she mean, four of them?" Hazel asked, turning to her mother for an answer.

Agnes shook her head. "I have no idea," she said. "All of the stories I have heard were only about the three. There was no mention of a fourth."

"It couldn't have been Patience Goodfellow," Rowan said, referring to Henry's ancestor who hid the grimoire away safely after the spell was cast. "It was someone who died with the sisters."

"The sisters didn't seem to place as much emphasis on the fourth soul as they did the fact that each of you need to find partners in this quest," Henry said. "Partners you can trust, who would be willing to sacrifice themselves for you."

He leaned over, took Rowan's hand in his and met her eyes. "I am your partner in this quest," he said solemnly. "I vow to do everything in my power to destroy the beast, even to the sacrifice of my own life."

Rowan leaned forward and kissed Henry gently on the lips. "I accept your vow with gratitude," she replied.

Joseph turned to Hazel, his face filled with dismay. "I would vow," he said to her, shaking his head. "But the fulfillment of the quest is not for several months, and I don't know..."

Hazel placed her hand over his mouth to stop him from finishing his sentence. "We will have to figure out

339

how to stop your curse," she said. "Because I know in my heart that you are my partner, and no one else will do."

He leaned over and kissed her. "You're right," he said softly, his eyes filled with love for her. "No one else will do."

Agnes watched a shadow of grief pass over Cat's features until she schooled them and took a deep breath. "Well, I would say that the first order of business is to cure Joseph," she said. "And we need to do it quickly."

Hazel sighed and shook her head. "Cat, it's not like he has a flu or something," she began.

Rowan's eyes widened, and then she reached over and hugged her sister. "Cat, you are brilliant," she said. "Quick, let's close this circle because I have an idea."

Henry grinned and turned to Joseph. "I have a feeling you're in for a wild ride."

"Those are the best kind," Joseph replied.

Chapter Fifty-two

Hazel entered Rowan's laboratory, put on a lab coat, slipped paper booties over her shoes, and walked toward the office.

"I still don't have a solution," Rowan called out to her sister from the confines of her office.

"It's been days," Hazel complained as she entered the office.

Rowan looked up from the computer screen she was studying and nodded sympathetically. "I know," she said. "But it takes a while for all of the genetic tests to process."

Hazel pulled a chair away from the counter and sat down next to Rowan, looking over her shoulder. "So, what do you have so far?" she asked.

"I think I've been able to isolate the mutation in his DNA when I compared it to his grandfather's DNA and to Gabriella's," Rowan said. "So, now the challenge is

341

how to get the corrected DNA to interact with his mutated DNA and correct the problem."

"Can you do that?" Hazel asked.

Rowan nodded. "When you mentioned that Joseph didn't have the flu the other day, it reminded me that viruses have the ability to affect DNA," she explained. "Not flu viruses, but viruses like HIV actually change someone's DNA. So, why not use that same idea to get rid of the mutated DNA strands and replace them with healthy ones?"

"Can that work?" Hazel asked.

"In theory it can," Rowan said. "And, actually, there is genetic research being done in labs all over the world to alter either genetics or DNA. The genetic alterations they've achieved don't seem to have the long-lasting affects we're looking for."

"But these tests are being done on mice, right?" Hazel assumed.

Rowan nodded her head. "Yes," she said. "There are a couple of small human studies, but nothing we could access."

"Okay, we think it can be done," Hazel said. "And we're running out of time. So, why don't we do something?"

"To actually correct the mutated DNA, we need someone with a close enough strand that's healthy to infiltrate Joseph's DNA," she said. "His grandfather's strand has a recessive genetic trait for the same disease. It wouldn't help him."

"So, you need someone with German DNA, right?" Hazel asked.

Rowan nodded. "Yeah, someone with roots that go back to the same region, Bavaria, as Joseph," she said.

Hazel shook her head. "This makes so much sense," she whispered, a look of amazement on her face.

"What?" Rowan asked.

"Me," she said. "My father was German. You need to test me."

Rowan's jaw dropped for a moment. "I never even considered…" she began. "But of course, the way things have just fallen into place with Henry and me, I should have thought of you and Joseph."

"What do you need?" Hazel asked. "Should I spit in a tube?"

Rowan grinned and shook her head. "No, I have your information," she said. "Remember when we were testing the machine when we first bought it? You spit in a tube a year ago." She turned back to her computer and accessed the files. "Okay, I'm running a comparison on you and Joseph. Cross your fingers."

Hazel shook her head. "I don't have to," she said. "All of this was set in motion before we were even born. I'll match Joseph. I know I will."

"I like your confidence," Rowan said. "And then there's the next problem."

"Okay, while you run your numbers," Hazel said, "let's solve that one."

"Easier said than done," Rowan replied. "How do we merge your healthy DNA with Joseph's unhealthy DNA?"

"When Cat had her vision, she saw Joseph, didn't she?" Hazel asked. "She saw you and Henry doing something in the clearing. Working together."

Rowan nodded and picked up her phone. "Hey Cat, can you come over to the lab?" she asked. "We really need your input on something."

Rowan hung up the phone and looked at Hazel. "She's on her way," she said.

"This has to work," Hazel said. "Because after this, we have to help Cat find her partner."

Chapter Fifty-three

"Sorry," Cat apologized as she entered the office, clothed in the same sterile garb as the others.

"Nice outfit," Hazel teased, looking at the shapeless, white lab coat.

Cat smiled at her sister. "Great shoes," she replied, acknowledging the light blue booties. "So, what's up?"

"The night we cast the circle," Rowan began, "you mentioned the vision you had that included Joseph. We need more details."

Cat nodded. "Okay, what do you need?" she asked.

"What were Rowan and Henry doing?" Hazel asked.

"Everyone was in a clearing," Cat recounted. "Rowan and Henry were standing together, their hands clasped, eyes closed, and they were working together. That was the impression I was given."

"So, they were healing someone, but they weren't touching anyone," Hazel said. "Isn't that odd?"

Rowan nodded slowly. "We weren't talking. Our eyes were closed, and we were forming a circle with our clasped hands," she repeated. "Was the clearing a cast circle?"

Cat closed her eyes for a moment and then nodded slowly. "It could have been," she said. "It was definitely a circle, but there was no protective light around it."

"Since it was outside, we could have dimmed the light," Hazel suggested.

"That's true," Cat agreed. "So, let's assume that it was a cast circle. Why is that important?"

"Well, if Henry and I were to astral project ourselves as healers," Rowan mused, "that would be the way we would do it."

"You can do that?" Hazel asked.

Rowan shrugged. "I have no idea," she said. "I've never tried it."

347

"But why would you even need to do that?" Hazel asked. "Why not just put your hands on Joseph and heal him?"

"It's not healing with the DNA strands," Rowan said. "It's more like directing. Like when we took the poison from Gabriella's body. We didn't heal her liver. We removed a foreign substance from it. It's kind of the same thing, but in reverse."

"You would have to put a strand of corrected DNA into his molecular structure," Cat said. "So, you'd be working on the cellular level of his anatomy. Can you do that?"

Rowan shrugged again. "I have no idea, once again," she admitted.

"But how do you get the right DNA into his body?" Cat asked. "If you are astral projecting in order to reach those basic structural components, you can't carry it in there with you."

Hazel turned to Cat. "In your vision, describe what you saw happening between Joseph and me," she requested.

Cat nodded. "Okay, this was a little odd," she said. "Joseph walked up to you and took both of your hands. Then you walked forward, got closer to him, and then, you were gone. But I knew you weren't gone. You were inside of him."

"Inside of him," Hazel repeated. "How the heck did I do that?"

"You can't astral project into him, because your spirit doesn't carry your DNA," Rowan said. "Somehow you would have to move your entire essence into his body."

"I don't think I can do that," Hazel said. "I mean, how would anyone do that?"

They sat in silence for a few moments, and then Cat turned to Hazel. "When you built the apartment over the barn, how did you move the materials from the warehouses to the barn?" she asked.

349

"I just pictured what I wanted and then kind of mentally searched for who had it. Then I pictured it where I wanted it and, blingo, it was there."

"See, that's why I can't do that kind of magic," Cat teased. "I don't know magic words like blingo."

Hazel turned to her oldest sister and stuck out her tongue. "Don't mock my choice of exclamatories."

Rowan, ignoring her sisters' conversation, was lost in thought. "Hazel," she said slowly. "Try picturing the kitchen in your mind."

"Okay," Hazel said with a shrug. "I'm picturing it."

"Now picture yourself in it," Rowan said. "And do your blingo thing."

Suddenly, Hazel disappeared from in front of them.

"Shouldn't we have set up some fail-safes before you sent your sister into the ether?" Cat demanded.

"I didn't realize…" Rowan stammered. "I didn't know…"

Suddenly Hazel appeared back in her seat with a cookie in her hand. "Now that was fun," she said, pulling two more cookies from her lab coat pocket and handing them to her sisters. "I haven't done that since high school."

"Wait. You've done that before?" Rowan asked.

Hazel opened her mouth, then shut it. "No," she finally said. "I've never done that before. I always stayed up in my room when I was grounded, especially if there was a party I wanted to go to."

"You are such a brat," Rowan said. "You never told me."

Hazel shrugged. "It was my superpower. I was like Clark Kent, only less buff," she replied.

"Okay, we have a solution," Cat said.

Hazel shook her head. "If I did that to Joseph, he'd probably explode."

Chapter Fifty-four

"No," Joseph said firmly, picking up a bale of straw and walking it over to the pen. "It's just not an option."

"But I've been practicing," Hazel pleaded, putting the pitchfork down for a moment. "I've been able to stay in this really awesome particle stage for five minutes."

"And what happens if you slip out of the particle stage?" he asked, placing the bale on the ground and peeling off his gloves.

She shrugged. "I'm pretty small, and you're pretty big," she said. "You could probably handle it."

"And you would suffocate because you'd be trapped inside me with no way to breath," he said. "No. We're not doing it."

"Rowan and Henry would be right there," she argued, "monitoring the whole thing, the whole time."

"And you can't even guarantee that it will work," he argued. "I'm not going to have you risk your life for something that might not even work."

She leaned the pitchfork against the pen and walked over to him. "So, let me make sure I have this straight," she said, her hands on her hips. "In the next few months, my family and I are going to have to face a demon of epic proportion. We are going to sacrifice everything we have in order to save the world, pretty much. We've been told that we can't do it alone, only with others who were foreordained to be our partners. And if we try to do it alone, we will probably die and not destroy the demon."

She stepped even closer and poked him in his chest with her finger. "You and I both agree that between the way we met and the fact that my DNA can potentially stop your death, that you were destined to be my partner in this quest." She shrugged. "I could be wrong. It could be Lefty, but I'm thinking it's you. But you aren't willing to let me help you in a slightly risky experiment because I

353

might have to hold my breath for a few minutes? You'd rather I wait and die by demon fire?"

"No," he said, shaking his head. "No, it's not like that."

"We have two days until the full moon," she said. "Two freaking days. You want me to sacrifice my whole family because you're afraid for me? Would you sacrifice your family if you were in the same situation?"

He sighed. "Hazel, you don't understand," he said.

She shook her head. "No, I don't," she interrupted. "We have the ability to save you. All we need is your permission."

"If you die, I'll never forgive myself," he said.

She rolled her eyes and poked his chest again. "If I die, you'll only have a couple more days to live," she said. "You'll get over it."

He sighed. "Hazel."

"Say yes," she said with determination, "because, that's the only answer I'll accept."

He placed his hands on her upper arms. "Can you promise…"

She shook her head. "I can't and won't promise anything," she said. "Because sometimes you just have to take a risk and move forward in faith."

He smiled at her. "My mom used to say that," he said.

"See, it's an old German saying," Hazel replied.

"My mom was Native American," he said.

"Borrowed from the Native Americans," she amended.

Chuckling, he bent forward and kissed her. "I love you, you know," he said softly.

She kissed him back. "Really, how could you resist?" she teased.

She slipped her hand into his and tugged gently. "Come on," she urged.

He shook his head and followed after her. "What? Where are we going?" he asked.

355

"To the clearing," she replied as they exited the barn. "To cure you."

"But your family…"

"Are all there waiting for us," she said, opening the pasture gate.

"But how did they know…"

She stopped, reached up and kissed him lightly again. "I told them that I wasn't going to give you any other option," she replied.

He planted his feet. "I don't think I like this," he said.

She met his eyes, all of the teasing gone from hers. "I would gladly die for you," she said sincerely. "And if something were to happen to you, I don't know how I would go on. But, I would, because I would need to stand with my family." She placed her hand on his arm. "But, if I have a choice, I would rather fight. I would rather fight for your life, fight for my family, and fight with you against the demon and win, so we can live happily ever after."

He pulled her to him and crushed his lips against hers. Then he stepped back and took a deep breath. "Let's fight."

Chapter Fifty-five

The woods were silent, except for a soft wind, and the stars were barely visible because the nearly full moon cast its bright glow on the fields and woods. The moon shadows of spindly branches flowed along the ground, dancing a willowy ballet as a corps de ballet of young trees bowed and swayed to the music of the wind. Hazel guided Joseph down a narrow path that finally opened up to a small, circular clearing.

"We love this place," she whispered.

He stepped inside the circle and looked around. Ancient oaks surrounded them like pillars in an ancient cathedral, their uppermost limbs intertwining overhead to create an arched dome that married the earth and the sky. He took a deep breath and turned to Hazel. "I smell candles," he replied, keeping his own voice soft as the sacredness of the place demanded it.

She smiled and nodded. "Cool, right?" she agreed quietly.

358

He noticed the rest of the family entering the clearing from the other side, and Hazel wrapped her arms around his arm and walked with him to the center.

"Well met," Agnes said, her voice deep and melodic. She turned to Joseph. "Do you accept this gift we offer you?"

He paused. He hadn't thought of it as a gift, but he suddenly realized it was. "Yes," he said. "With gratitude."

Agnes smiled and nodded. "Then we will begin."

The four Willoughby women stepped back from the center, each to one compass point in the circle, and cleaned the area as they had done in their own circle at home. But this time they didn't use smudge sticks. Instead, they used long rods of crystal to perform the ritual. The energy inside the circle felt the same, like the air after a lightning storm, and Joseph and Henry watched and waited for them to finish.

Finally, when they stepped back into the center of the circle, the edge of the clearing glowed softly but was not as bright as it had been inside their home. However, the ancient oak trees also glowed with golden power, and their limbs were now interwoven, creating a wall of leaves around them.

"Joseph, please kneel in the center of the circle," Agnes directed. "Hazel, you kneel in front of him. Rowan and Henry, stand on either side of Joseph, and Cat, you and I will stand on either side of Hazel."

Joseph knelt and watched Hazel kneel in front of him. "Are you sure…" he asked softly.

She smiled and nodded. "Faith, remember?" she whispered back.

Rowan and Henry stood on either side of him and offered reassuring smiles. Then Cat and Agnes took their places. "Are we ready?" Agnes asked.

Everyone nodded.

"Hazel, you begin," Agnes directed.

Hazel closed her eyes and began her spell:

"In this sacred, guarded site,

I wish to shift within thy light,

To be myself, yet distinct and free.

As I wish, so mote it be."

Hazel disappeared, and Agnes nodded. "Rowan, Henry, quickly," she said.

Rowan reached over Joseph and clasped Henry's hands. "See you on the inside," she said with a smile. Then she began the spell:

"To heal a wound that lies deep inside,

We ask for power to be astral guides."

Henry closed his eyes and finished:

"Two becomes one, resolve and remedy,

 Life is renewed, so mote it be."

 Suddenly they were inside of Joseph, surrounded by his internal organs. "I think it worked," Rowan said, looking over at Henry. "Let's go to his heart."

"I can hear you, but I can't see you," Hazel said.

"That's okay," Henry said. "We can feel your presence, so we'll be able to help move things around once we get to his heart."

"I can hear you too," Joseph said, his voice rumbling throughout his body. "And I have to admit it's weird."

Hazel laughed softly. "I'm sure it is," she said.

"Hazel, I need you to try and overlay his organs," Rowan said.

"Just guide me, and I'll go," she said.

Henry and Rowan saw the microscopic pieces of Hazel, unformed and floating, next to Joseph's organs. "Slide slightly to the left," Rowan said. "Now down, just a bit. Stop! Good. Can you just rest there?"

Hazel felt a strange shift in power and warmth in her own body. "Is it working?" she asked.

"I can feel your heartbeat," Joseph whispered in awe. "I can feel your heart against my own."

"Just another moment," Henry said. "We're combining the DNA strands, and they seem to be connecting well."

"Of course they are," Hazel said, feeling strange pulses of energy in her own body.

"I'm going to increase the conversion process," Rowan said, "so the changes we've implemented today move faster than usual in order to be sure the strands are more mature in two days."

"Thank you," Joseph replied.

Rowan wove her spell:

"Two were merged to correct a wrong,

The renewal of life now becomes strong.

Escalate the process from what occurs normally,

To protect and heal, so mote it be."

Hazel felt another energy surge inside of her. "It feels like something's working in there," she said.

"Yes, it looks good," Henry said. "Hazel, you can slide out now."

"Okay," Hazel replied.

"In this sacred, guarded site,

I wish to shift within thy light,

To return to the human form of me.

As I wish, so mote it be."

Hazel appeared in front of Joseph, and he immediately pulled her into his arms. "Are you okay?" he asked.

She nodded. "It was great," she said. "I didn't think that I would feel the changes, but I did. I kept feeling energy and warmth, like my body was affected by it too. How do you feel?"

"Like there's been a party in my body," he teased, then bent forward and kissed her. "Thank you."

Rowan and Henry opened their eyes and unclasped their hands.

"I think we did it," Rowan said. "When we left, Hazel's DNA strands were multiplying and eradicating the mutated gene."

"When will we know for sure?" Hazel asked.

Henry sighed. "Not until the full moon," he said. Then he turned to Joseph. "Rowan increased your body's metabolism, so there might be strange side effects. But it won't last too long, just until it heals itself."

Joseph stood up, reached down and helped Hazel to her feet. She stood up and then clasped onto his arms because she felt lightheaded. "Are you all right?" he asked.

"Just lightheaded," she said with a shrug. "I guess hanging around in someone's body takes more energy than I'm used to."

"Can you walk?" Joseph asked.

"Yes, I'm fine," she assured him, but was grateful when he put his arm around her and let her rest against him.

"Let's close the circle," Agnes said. "And then we can go home."

Hazel bit back a yawn and nodded. "Home sounds really good."

Chapter Fifty-six

Once they got back to the Willoughby house, they sat around the kitchen table, celebrating with herb tea and cookies.

"Thank you for all you've done for me," Joseph said.

"Don't thank us yet," Henry said. "Not until the morning after the full moon."

He looked down and smiled softly at Hazel, snuggled against his side and sleeping peacefully. "This has really taken a lot out of her."

Cat studied her youngest sister. "I'm really surprised she's this tired," she said.

"Maybe it's just the relief after so much stress," Agnes suggested. "Poor dear."

"If it works, I know she'd say it was more than worth it," Rowan said.

Joseph looked from Hazel to Rowan. "If this works, do you think you could replicate it?" he asked. "Without endangering Hazel?"

Rowan nodded. "Yes, we can use samples of Hazel's DNA and create a vaccine for the boys in your village," she said. "And, if we could do more research with samples, we might be able to alter the DNA in the girls too, so the problem isn't passed on. But mostly, you really need to expand the gene pool."

"Stop hiding from the outside world, you mean?" Joseph asked.

"Yes, exactly," Rowan said. "I don't think the danger you faced in the past is realistic any longer."

"You believe people are more understanding?" Joseph asked.

Henry shrugged. "Actually, I think people are just as prejudiced about things they don't understand as they were in the past, speaking anthropologically," he said. "But I also think that there are tools at your disposal that your village could learn to use to contain your secret and still allow you all to interact with society."

"Whether or not it's safe," Rowan said, "now it's a matter of survival. Do you think your grandfather will be open to the idea?"

"I'm going to go see him tonight," Joseph said. "And tell him about what you did for me." He looked down at Hazel and lowered his voice. "Even if what we did tonight doesn't work, I'd like you to keep working on a solution for the others in my village."

Henry nodded. "We promise we will," he said. "But we're really counting on you to be our first success story."

Joseph smiled. "Thank you. I'd like that too," he said. He turned to Agnes. "May I carry Hazel up to her room before I leave?"

She nodded. "Yes, it's the bedroom at the top on the right," she said.

He turned slightly, so she slid against his chest, and then he slipped both arms underneath her and stood up. She didn't wake up, just snuggled closer and snored slightly.

A little concerned, he turned back to Agnes. "Will you check on her later and call me if she needs anything?" he asked.

Agnes nodded, smiling indulgently. "Of course I will," she said. "Thank you, Joseph."

They watched the giant of a man carry the petite Hazel out of the room and carefully up the stairs.

"He obviously doesn't understand motherhood," Rowan whispered with a smile, "if he thought for an instant that you would go to bed without checking on her."

Agnes shook her head. "No, he doesn't understand motherhood," she agreed. "But he is totally smitten, isn't he?"

Henry nodded. "I completely understand the feeling," he said, leaning over to give Rowan a kiss.

"What are the odds this is going to work?" Cat asked, concerned for Hazel's heart.

"From what we could see, his body was accepting the strands," Rowan replied. "Unless we missed something, he should be fine."

Chapter Fifty-seven

Joseph drove from the Willoughby farm to the hidden road near his village. He hid his car and walked down the path to the secreted entrance and slipped inside. The village was dark, with no candlelight gleaming from the windows of the homes, but the light from the nearly full moon was enough for Joseph to make his way down the familiar streets to the church. He climbed up the steps and began to push the door open when it was opened for him.

Henrich, tears of joy in his eyes, embraced Joseph. "I am so glad to see you," he whispered hoarsely. "Thank you for coming to see me."

"Of course I would come," Joseph replied, moved by the love of his grandfather. "Nothing would have stopped me. But I come with good news."

"You have found Helga?" Henrich asked.

Joseph shook his head. "No, I haven't. I searched for miles, and there is no sign nor scent of her. I'm afraid she was able to get a ride somewhere."

"Well, that doesn't matter," Henrich said. "Tell me your good news."

"The Willoughbys think they have found a cure for our Rumspringa curse," he said. "It is in our DNA, a mutation that causes death or permanent change."

"So, what does that mean, if it is in our DNA?" he asked.

"It means there may be a cure for it," Joseph said. "Tonight, we tried the initial cure on me."

Henrich's face filled with joy. "And it worked?" he asked with excitement.

Joseph shrugged. "We won't know until the full moon," he said. "But, grandfather, even if it does not work, I want you to help the Willoughbys find a cure for the other men and boys in our village. Promise me you will work with them and help them."

Henrich studied Joseph and then hugged him again. "And what else is bothering you that you cannot say to me?" he asked.

"If I do not make it," he said, "I need a promise from you."

"I do not make a promise until I know what it entails," Henrich replied. "Even from you."

"You will not like what I ask," Joseph replied. "But, I still ask it. On the night of the full moon there will be a ceremony honoring a demon. The Willoughbys have been sworn to fight the demon."

"I know of this," Henrich said. "This legend of the Willoughby Witches."

"The time is soon that the demon will be released," Joseph explained. "But this, this full moon is not the release. It is the time when those who honor and support the demon come together to give him more power and perhaps get more power themselves."

"This sounds like a dangerous time for the Willoughbys," Henrich said.

"If I am not there to protect them, I ask you to come to their aid," Joseph said. "Not only because…"

"Because you love the little one, Miss Willoughby," Henrich said gently.

Joseph nodded. "Not only because I will not be there to defend Hazel," he said, his voice raw, "but also because they can save our village. And they will."

"They have already saved us," Henrich said. "We already owe a debt. We will help. Where is this ceremony to be?"

"I don't know," Joseph said. "In the woods, secreted away."

"Don't worry," Henrich promised. "We will do all we can to protect them." He put his hand on Joseph's shoulder. "Come inside. I have something for you."

Joseph paused. "I really should be getting back to town," he said.

Henrich patted his shoulder and shook his head. "No, you come inside first, and then you can go back to your job."

Joseph followed Henrich into the church and through the chapel. Henrich looked over at the angels over the altar and chuckled deeply. "I still laugh at your little angel, Hazel," he said. "Was there ever such a one?"

Joseph smiled. "No, I think she is totally unique," he agreed. "Which is probably a good thing."

Henrich laughed. "Yes," he agreed. "Yes, it is a good thing."

Leading him down the hallway, Henrich entered his study. He walked across the room to a picture on the wall and pulled the picture forward to expose a wall safe hidden behind it. He turned the combination lock and in a matter of moments, the safe opened. Then he reached inside and pulled out a small box.

"This box," he said, placing it in Joseph's hand and then placing his hand on top of it, "holds the ring I gave your grandmother. I would like you to give it to your Hazel."

"But if I don't—" Joseph began.

"It doesn't matter," Henrich interrupted. "She has your heart. She should have this ring."

"Thank you, grandfather," Joseph said. "I will give it to her and I know she will treasure it."

"Tell her, no matter what," Henrich said, "she is now my granddaughter."

His voice silenced with emotion, Joseph just stepped forward and hugged his grandfather. Finally, he was able to speak through his tears. "I love you, Grandfather," he whispered.

"And I love you, my Joseph," he replied. "And I will pray that the Willoughbys' magic will work."

"Thank you," Joseph said. "Hazel said I must have faith." He stepped back and smiled at Henrich. "So, I will see you in three days' time, and I will bring Hazel here to visit."

"Good," Henrich said, whisking away his tears. "That is very good."

Chapter Fifty-eight

Hazel slowly came down the steps into the kitchen the next morning, moaning softly and holding her stomach. "I feel like I'm going to die," she said, walking over to the cookie jar and pulling out an oatmeal raisin cookie.

Rowan turned and shook her head. "You're going to die, and you're eating cookies?" she asked skeptically,

Hazel nibbled on the cookie. "I have to keep my strength up," she said, walking over to the cabinet and pulling down a mug. "And an oatmeal cookie is the only thing that sounds good."

Rowan walked over and placed her hand on her sister's forehead. "Well, you don't have a fever," she said.

"That's good to know," Hazel whimpered. Then she met Rowan's eyes. "I have a question for you, and I want you to be honest with me."

"Of course," Rowan replied. "What?"

"Is there any chance that yesterday when I was giving my DNA to Joseph, he could have been giving his DNA to me?" she asked.

Rowan stared at her sister in wide-eyed horror. "I never even thought of that possibility," she said, dismayed. "Oh, Hazel, if anything…"

Hazel waved her hand at her sister to silence her. "No! Wait! Stop!" she insisted. "Even if there are ramifications, I would do this all over again for the chance that we could save Joseph's life. And, as I recall, I was the one who was pushing for a quick solution. So, you know, no harm, no foul. But I just don't want to be totally surprised if I wake up and I'm a wolf or something like that."

Rowan reached over, took her own cookie out of the jar and bit down with a vengeance. "Okay," she said as she chewed. "Let me think about this. Your DNA was stronger and seemed to overpower the mutated cell in Joseph's DNA."

Hazel took another nibble of her cookie and then poured hot water into her tea cup. "So, the mutation part is out," Hazel said. "And, besides, the girls didn't die, just the guys."

Rowan nodded and pointed at Hazel with her cookie. "Right! Good, yes," she said. "Only the men, Y chromosomes, had the death thingie."

"I love it when you're technical like that," Hazel said. "Death thingie."

"Don't interrupt me when I'm thinking," Rowan said, taking another bite. "Okay, so is wolf a dominant or recessive genetic trait?"

"Is that a rhetorical question?" Hazel asked.

"I'm just thinking out loud," Rowan said. "And if it's recessive, do we have any genetic traits that would push it into a dominant trait?"

"Like do wolf and witchcraft equal, I don't know, Bigfoot?" Hazel asked.

"Right!" Rowan replied.

"I so don't want to become a Bigfoot," Hazel said, slumping into a chair. "I already hate shaving my legs. Can you imagine?"

"It would have to be a wax job," Rowan said. "A whole-body wax job."

"You are really a mean person," Hazel said, sipping on her tea. "Everyone thinks you're so nice and intellectual, but no, you have a mean streak a mile wide."

Rowan went over and hugged her sister. "Don't worry," she said. "I still have complete samples of your DNA, so there's a chance we can repair what we did."

"And maybe I just have a cold," Hazel said hopefully. "Or the flu. Or something equally as potent, but harmless."

Rowan nodded. "And maybe, while you were in Joseph's body, you picked up a latent virus he had swimming around his body. And since you didn't also pick up his antibodies, you got sick."

Hazel nodded and smiled at her sister. "Okay, let's go with that one," she said. "It's just a bug. It's just the flu. I'm going to get better soon."

"And just to make up for teasing you, I'll milk the goats this morning," she said. "And Henry will clean the pens."

Hazel chuckled. "Oh, I know Henry's going to love that," she replied. "Thank you, sis."

"Hey, that's what sisters are for," she said. "Go back to bed and get some rest."

Chapter Fifty-nine

Joseph was surprised to find Donovan waiting for him in his office when he got there the next morning.

"Hmmm," Joseph said casually as he closed the door behind him and locked it. "I was sure I was the only one with keys to my office."

He walked over to his credenza and turned on the music. A selection from the opera "The Pirates of Penzance" began to play.

Donovan nodded approvingly. "Nice," he said.

"One of my favorites," Joseph replied.

Donovan looked over his shoulder from the chair he was sitting in and raised a Styrofoam cup. "I brought you coffee," he said.

Joseph slipped around the desk, picked up the cup, and stared at it for a moment. "How do I know it's not poisoned?" he asked.

"Oh, good grief," Donovan replied. "Why would I want to poison you?"

"Because of the mosq…I mean the Master," Joseph replied, sitting back in his chair and leaving the coffee on his desk. "What can I do for you?"

"How are the Willoughbys doing?" Donovan asked.

Joseph studied him for a long moment and then shook his head. "See, what we have here is a simple trust issue," he finally said. "You don't trust me enough to tell me which side you're really on, and I don't trust you enough to give you any details about the Willoughbys that can be used against them."

Donovan nodded. "So, is that why you didn't tell me you are a werewolf?" he asked.

Joseph didn't allow himself to react to the question. Instead he met Donovan's eyes steadily and slowly nodded his head. "Because I'm not," he said. "Care to try again?"

"Mayor Bates has a new friend who swears that you are a werewolf," Donovan said.

"Helga is with Bates," Joseph said slowly. "Well, damn."

"You know her?" Donovan asked.

"Yeah, she is wanted for attempted murder in the village of Wulffolk," he said. "It's a small village a couple of miles away from here."

"I never heard of it," Donovan said.

Joseph shrugged. "You wouldn't have," he said. "They are like the Amish. They don't use modern conveniences, and they don't really interact with others. Helga was a villager who was caught poisoning children."

"Did she have a gingerbread house too?" Donovan asked.

Joseph allowed a smile to spread on his face. "Now, see, that would be a wicked witch, like you," he said. "A werewolf wouldn't be into that whole baking thing."

"Wulffolk, huh?" Donovan asked. "Wolf people?"

"So, did you and Hazel take German classes together?" Joseph asked.

384

"What?" Donovan questioned.

Joseph chuckled and shook his head. "Never mind," he said. "The people are from a small county in Bavaria called Wulffolk. But if you want to pretend there are monsters in the woods, who am I to stop you?"

"Are you lying to me?" Donovan asked.

"Look it up," Joseph replied casually and then decided to change the subject. "Have you found out where the ceremony is going to be held on the night of the full moon?"

Donovan shook his head. "No, they haven't told me," he said. "But I'm even more concerned about it."

"Why?"

"I overheard something about a blood sacrifice," he said. "I don't know what they have in mind, but please make sure the Willoughbys' goats are put away and protected before nightfall."

Joseph nodded. "Losing one of those goats would break Hazel's heart," he agreed. Then he sat up as another thought came into his mind. "They aren't thinking about sacrificing a person, are they?"

"No," Donovan replied. Then he paused. "At least I don't think so. It seems to me that Bates is becoming a little more unstable every day." He leaned forward in his chair and lowered his voice. "You have protection for them, right?"

Joseph nodded. "I do," he said. "But if you can be there to help, that wouldn't be a bad thing."

Donovan sighed and shook his head. "I don't think I can do that," he said. "I need to make an appearance at the ceremony."

"You know you're playing a dangerous game," Joseph said. "And not just with your own life, with the Willoughbys too."

Donovan stood up. "I'm just doing what I think is the right thing to do," he said.

"Just don't do anything stupid," Joseph said.

Donovan smiled. "Thanks for the advice," he replied wryly.

Joseph shrugged. "Best advice I ever got," he said. "Be careful out there."

Donovan nodded and then left the office. When he closed the door behind him, Joseph picked up the coffee and tossed it in the garbage. "I'm not quite ready to trust you," he murmured. "With my life or the Willoughbys."

Chapter Sixty

The next night, as Hazel finished with the goats, she heard a knock on the barn door.

"Come in," she called.

Joseph opened the door, walked inside, and then closed it behind him. "Are we alone?" he asked, hiding his hands behind his back.

She smiled at him, feeling her love bursting inside. "Well, except for the goats," she replied.

"Good," he said, stepping forward. He pulled one hand out from behind his back and handed her a bouquet of flowers.

"Oh, they are so beautiful," she said, her heart melting. She lowered her face and breathed in their fragrance. "And they smell so good. Thank you."

She rose up and brushed a kiss over his lips.

He put the flowers down on a stack of hay bales and took her into his arms. "I have to admit," he said with a regretful shake of his head, "they are from Gabriella and

388

not from me. I went to see her in the village today. She is

so much better. She is racing around with all of the other

children."

"Oh, that's wonderful," she said, and then she

added with a teasing smile. "But, since they are from

Gabriella and not you, you have to give me back my kiss."

He lowered his face until they were only inches

apart. "With pleasure," he whispered, and then he

captured her lips with his. He deepened the kiss, pouring

all of his emotion into it. When he stepped back, her eyes

were filled with tears.

"What?" he asked, worried.

"That was a goodbye kiss," she whispered, and

then she shook her head. "I don't want a goodbye kiss."

He pulled her into his arms and held her. "I don't

want it to be a goodbye kiss either," he said. "But I don't

know what tonight will bring."

"I want to wait with you," she said.

"What? No!" he said, stepping back and looking

down at her. "It's too dangerous. The ceremony for the

389

other coven is tonight, and we don't know where they're going to be. And I don't know what's going to happen to me, how I'm going to react."

"I need to be there," she insisted. "I need to know what happens to you."

"Hazel, please," he said. "This might be our last time together. Please don't argue with me."

"Okay, a compromise," she said.

"What?" he asked.

"We have a picnic, together, here in the barn," she said. "I'll be safe. We can wait for the full moon together, and I'll know what happens."

"But you haven't been feeling well," he said. "You need your rest."

"I'm feeling much better today," she replied, crossing her fingers surreptitiously behind her back. "Besides, I won't be able to rest because I'll be worrying about you."

He nodded. "Okay," he agreed. "A picnic would be wonderful, and it's a beautiful night to enjoy it."

She smiled at him. "We can have it on the balcony," she suggested.

"I didn't know you had a balcony," he replied.

"Well, we didn't until just now," she said. "But it's going to be perfect."

They locked the goats in their pens and secured all of the windows and doors. Hazel led the way across the barn, on the opposite side from Henry's apartment, and up the loft steps to a latched door.

"Ready?" she asked.

He shook his head. "I don't think I'm ever ready when I'm dealing with you," he admitted.

She laughed with delight and then opened the door, leading the way outside. The small balcony was strewn with tiny, white lights and fragrant, white flowers. A small, glass table and two chairs took up the center of the balcony, and in a vase in the middle of the table was the bouquet from Gabriella.

Joseph shook his head. "This is perfect," he said.

She turned and smiled at him. "Perfect for what?" she asked.

He pulled the small box out of his pocket and knelt down on one knee.

Hazel's eyes widened and filled with tears. She covered her mouth with her hands.

"Hazel, I don't know what tonight is going to bring," Joseph said. "But I know I can't leave this earth without telling you how much I love you and without giving you this."

He opened up the box, and the dainty, gold filigree ring studded with diamonds sparkled in the night sky.

"Oh, Joseph, it's beautiful," she whispered through her tears.

"It was my grandmother's ring," he said. "And now it belongs to you, if you'll accept it."

She slowly knelt before him and held out her hand. "I love you, Joseph," she breathed softly. "Of course I'll accept it."

He slipped the ring on her finger, then leaned forward and kissed her. She wrapped her arms around his neck and kissed him back, pouring all of her love into it. He wrapped his arms around her waist and crushed her to him. When their kiss had ended, he continued to hold her.

"I don't know what tonight is going to bring," he whispered in her ear. "So, I'm not going to hold you to a pledge that may never come to be."

She pulled back and gently placed her hand over his lips. "Joseph, I love you," she said simply. "Only you. There will never be another love for me. I pledge my heart, my life, and my love to you."

He took a deep breath and nodded slowly. "Hazel, will you marry me?" he asked.

She smiled at him. "Oh, yes," she breathed, throwing her arms around him again. "Oh, yes, I will."

Chapter Sixty-one

An hour later, the table and chairs were replaced with a love seat. The tiny lights were turned off, and Hazel was wrapped in Joseph's arms. She leaned against his chest and sighed with happiness.

"Everyone is thrilled with our announcement," she said, glancing at her phone and then sliding it into her back pocket. "I told them that we'd come in later, that we want to watch the moon together."

He chuckled softly. "We haven't been watching the moon," he reminded her, placing another kiss on her lips and then looking down into her eyes. "But, quite honestly, I prefer this view."

"This is perfect," she said.

He leaned down, placed a kiss on her head and shook his head. "You are perfect," he said.

She snorted. "Hardly," she replied. "But our life is going to be perfect. I can picture us in a cute little cottage with a big yard."

He adjusted his arms, pulling her closer, and laid his head against hers. "And cute little puppies all over the place," he said.

She pulled away and stared at him. "Are your children, I mean, our children going to be puppies?" she asked, aghast.

He laughed so hard that he nearly dislodged her from her place against his chest. "No," he finally breathed, wiping the tears from his eyes. "No, our babies will not be puppies. They will be regular babies. I just happen to like dogs."

She breathed a sigh of relief and settled back against him. "Well, me too," she said with a smile. "And goats, we have to have goats."

He lowered his head and kissed her deeply. "And children," he finally said. "Lots of children."

She nodded and kissed him back. "Okay, let's have a little boy first," she sighed.

He looked down at her. "You can do that?" he asked.

"What? Have babies?" she responded. "I think so."

"No," he said, shaking his head. "Choose which kind you have."

She grinned and shook her head. "No, I can't," she teased. "Don't you know anything about genetics? The dad is responsible for the sex of the baby."

"Okay, then," he said with a firm nod. "Then we should have a girl first, and she should look just like you."

She looked up at him and smiled. "And she will have you wrapped around her tiny, little finger from the moment she's born," she whispered.

He leaned down and kissed her again. "Just like her mother does," he said. Then his expression changed, and he grimaced.

"What?" she asked.

He glanced up at the sky. "The moon," he said, groaning. "It's nearing its apex."

She sat up and put her hands on his shoulders. "What does that mean?" she asked, frightened.

396

He looked at her, regret in his eyes. "I'm changing," he said. "I feel it coming on."

She shook her head. "No, we fixed that," she said. "You're going to be fine. We're going to be married."

He took a deep breath, and she felt his body ripple beneath her. "Can we stop it?" she asked.

"I love you, Hazel," he said. "Even if I don't remember when I change, know that deep in my heart I'll always love you."

He gently moved her away from him and stood up.

Tears flowed down her cheeks. "Joseph, don't leave me," she cried softly.

He turned to her just as the final steps of his transformation occurred and his face elongated. "I love—," the last word was lost in a long howl. Then Joseph leapt off the balcony and bounded into the woods.

Hazel stumbled to the edge of the balcony and watched him until he was lost from view. "Remember me, Joseph," she pleaded. "Remember me."

Chapter Sixty-two

Drying her eyes on a linen napkin, Hazel pushed
open the door that led to the barn and walked onto the loft.
The lights were dim, and she had to watch her step to
ensure she didn't trip on a corner of a hay bale. The goats
were a little restless, but that wasn't unusual for a night
with a full moon. *Everyone, it seems*, she thought sadly, *is
affected by the moon in way or another.*

She started down the steps and noticed a figure
down below. "Who's there?" she asked, pausing at the
top.

A lantern switched on, and Harley, her old friend
from the feed store, stepped forward. "I'm so sorry,
Hazel," he apologized. "I was supposed to come find you.
But I didn't mean to frighten you."

"Harley," she said with relief, continuing down
the stairs. "What are you doing here this late at night? I
don't need anything from the…"

She was surprised when she felt something cold and heavy surround her wrist as she stepped off the staircase.

"I'm so sorry, Hazel," Harley repeated. Then he jerked her backwards and caught her other wrist in the handcuffs behind her back. "These are iron. So, you know, don't struggle or anything."

"Harley?" Hazel cried, confused. "What are you doing?"

He grabbed hold of the chain that connected the cuffs and pushed his fist into the small of her back. "Just come along quietly," he said. "I would hate to use my gun."

"Your gun?" she breathed, shocked.

"The Master only wanted you," he explained. "But he said if I needed, I could shoot any of your family members that tried to stop me."

"But, Harley, you were always my friend," Hazel pleaded. "I've never done anything to you. Please don't do this."

"It's nothing personal, Hazel," he said, slowly guiding her out of the barn and behind the pens. "Nothing personal at all. And, if you think about it, it's kind of an honor."

"An honor?" Hazel asked, chilled at the casual horror of his words.

"Yes, an honor," he repeated. "The Master needs a virgin for tonight's ceremony, and you were chosen."

He pushed her down into the ditch near the road, and she stumbled in the high grass and weeds. "Be careful there," he said. "We don't want you getting hurt."

"Harley, you have to let me go," she said. "They're going to kill me. You don't want to be a part of this."

Harley sighed. "You know, at first that's what I thought, that I just didn't want to be a part of this," he replied, pushing her up onto the gravel road. "But, you know, once I realized how much good the Master was going to do for the people of Whitewater, I felt it was my duty to be part."

"He's not going to do good, Harley," Hazel argued. "He's lying to you. He's lying to all of you."

"See, that's where you're wrong, Hazel," he said easily. "He already got me two big contracts that I never thought I could get. My business is better than ever. It's like blessings."

"It's not blessings," Hazel said. "It's a lie. It's all a lie. Harley, can you really let me get killed over a couple big contracts?"

Harley sighed. "Well, if it were just me, I'd say no," he rationalized. "But, you know, I got employees I've got to take care of. I've got mouths to feed."

He pulled her to a stop next to his big delivery truck. "Step on up, Hazel," he said, opening the back of the truck.

When she hesitated, she felt the cold barrel of his gun against her back. "I would hate to kill you right here, Hazel," he said with a little regret. "And, you know, if I kill you, then I've got to go back to your house and get one of your sisters. So, you come with me and they'll be safe."

She had no choice. It was her life for the lives of her family. "I'll step up, Harley," she said. "Leave my family out of it."

"I thought you'd say that," he replied. "You were always such a good person, Hazel. It's a shame. It's really a shame."

He hooked the chain of her handcuffs to a larger cable that was attached to the wall of the truck. There were about a dozen feed sacks stacked around the floor of the truck. "I tried to make it so it was comfortable for you," he said. "But it won't be a long ride either way."

He closed the door, and Hazel was plunged into darkness. Hazel slid her phone out of her back pocket and pressed it on.

The roar of the truck hid her phone assistant's voice as it asked Hazel what she wanted.

"Call Mom," Hazel replied.

"Calling Mom," the phone replied.

"Hazel?" Agnes asked. "What's wrong?"

"They're taking me to the ceremony," she called. "I'm in iron handcuffs. Harley has me in his delivery truck. He's armed. He has a gun."

"We're on our way," Agnes said. "Where's Joseph?"

Tears spilled out of Hazel's eyes. "I don't know," she whispered. "I don't know."

Chapter Sixty-three

Joseph raced down the narrow paths between the trees, his footpads falling silently on the dirt and grass. His eyes were alert, looking for prey or predator, because survival was his only goal. He could hear the rustle of rodents under the leaves, the crash of raccoons through the brush, and the soft thump of owl wings as they gained height in the night's sky. In the distance he could hear the rumble of a truck on the road, and even farther away, the sounds of a freight train moving across the plains.

Freedom! He inhaled deeply and opened his mouth to taste it, panting with excitement. Freedom. A lone alpha, the world was his territory, and he had no boundaries, no worries, no family. He stumbled forward in his run.

Family.

The wolfman paused and cocked his head, bewildered by the inner confusion he was feeling. He lifted his head and howled again, a song of his freedom.

Yet, the song sounded different to him. Not freedom, but loneliness.

He looked back at the path he'd been running and shook his head.

There was nothing back there. There was only the path ahead, only the journey beyond, only the next kill or the next fight. Only…

He scratched at the ground, impatient with himself. Move on. But something, some internal leash was holding him back. And then he heard it. As his heart beat rapidly in his chest from the exertion of the run, he heard an answering heartbeat. He breathed slowly, intent on hearing the inner workings of his body. It was there, echoing softly, beating with his own, yet unique—another heart, a companion heart.

He looked up, and brown eyes turned amber.

"Hazel," he whispered softly.

"Hazel!" he yelled.

He turned and ran back down the path, the graceful lope of the wolf slowly becoming the athletic run of a man. "Hazel," he called to the night sky. "I

remembered."

Chapter Sixty-four

The truck stopped with a jolt, and Hazel was nearly thrown off the feed sacks she'd been sitting on. Her stomach reeled, both from the overwhelming smell of the feed and the roughness of the ride. Harley opened the back door, and Hazel lurched to her feet.

"Hey, wait a second," he said, alarmed. "I got to..."

But she had already leaned out of the back of the truck and spilled the contents of her stomach on the ground.

"Are you sick?" Harley asked. "I don't know if the Master wants a sick sacrifice."

"Water," Hazel croaked.

Harley nodded. "Oh, yeah, I got some upfront," he said. "Just a sec."

Hazel, still attached to her iron tether, looked out the truck door and gasped. There were at least a hundred people milling around the bluff, all dressed in dark clothing. This was not the coven she remembered. This was huge.

"Impressed by our little community?"

Hazel looked down in surprise. "Mayor Bates?" she asked. "You are part of this?"

"I lead this," he said. "Under the direction of the Master, I am in command."

"He's lying to you," she said, her throat raw. "He's using you."

"Of course, you'd say that," Bates replied. "Your family will lose power if he is allowed to go free."

She shook her head. "No, that's not true," she said. "He's afraid of our power."

"He's not afraid of anything," Bates exclaimed. "Least of all you."

He stepped away from the truck and turned towards the cab. "Harley, what the hell is taking you so long?" he yelled.

Harley came around the other side with a bottle of water in his hands. "Here," he said, handing the bottle in Hazel's direction.

"My hands are cuffed," Hazel said. "You're going to have to help me, unless you'd like to uncuff me."

He held the water to her lips and let her drink. She sipped, swished the water in her mouth, turned her head and spit the water in the direction of the mayor. A stream of water hit his back, and he yelled, "What the hell?"

Hazel met his eyes boldly.

"She's sick," Harley inserted, stepping between Hazel and Bates. "Are you sure you want her if she's sick?"

Bates narrowed his eyes and stared back at Hazel. "Oh, yes," he said. "I'm sure."

Then he turned to Harley. "Bring her up to the top of the bluff."

Harley unhooked the cable in the truck and guided Hazel down onto the ground. "You could let me go," she

410

whispered to Harley. "You could tell them I got loose. It wouldn't be your fault."

Harley glanced over at her, his eyes filled with doubt. "I don't know," he began. "I thought this would be a good thing."

"You've known me since I was a little girl," Hazel pleaded. "You helped me in 4-H. Harley, just drop your hand, and I'll run."

Sweat beaded on his forehead, and he glanced around. "I don't know," he whispered.

"You don't know what?" Helga exclaimed as she came up beside them. She was dressed in a dress of all black, her black hair up in a bun. "Was this witch trying to convince you to betray the Master?"

Harley shook his head. "No. No," he said. "I don't think so."

"I'll escort her," Helga snapped, pulling the chain from Harley's hand and yanking Hazel's arms backwards. "There's no way this bitch is going to talk me out of watching her die."

Chapter Sixty-five

Cat opened her eyes and turned to Henry, who was driving the Jeep. "They're up on the bluff above the lake," she said. "Take this road to the left."

Henry shifted gears and took the turn at full speed, the tires spitting up gravel as he rounded the curve. "How far up?" he asked.

"Another two miles," Cat said. "But I don't think we should take the Jeep all the way up. People will recognize us."

"Is there a dirt road we can take?" he asked.

"No," Rowan said. "Everything else is too rocky, even with four-wheel drive."

"Okay, I'll keep going up until you tell me to stop," he said, accelerating up the winding road.

"There's an outcropping in about a mile," Agnes said. "We can park the Jeep there and go up through the woods without anyone seeing us."

Henry pulled the Jeep into a narrow parking place, put it in gear and then turned it off. They all quickly climbed out of the Jeep, and Fuzzy led the way to the path. The full moon lit the path for the most part, but shadows from the large trees above darkened several long stretches of ground.

"Be careful," Agnes warned, keeping her voice low. "The drop off is treacherous."

"Isn't there anything we can do now?" Henry asked as they hurried up the slope.

Agnes shook her head. "We just have to pray we get there in time."

Cat stepped away from the path for a moment and closed her eyes. With Hazel's life in danger, she decided it was worth the risk. She reached out into the ether and searched for Donovan. Finally, she felt a connection. "The coven has Hazel," she sent to his mind. "They kidnapped her for the ceremony. We need your help."

She waited, but nothing was sent back. "He's not going to help," she whispered, the pain piercing her heart. He really was on the other side.

Wiping any tears from her eyes, she stepped back onto the path and caught up with the others. They were now near the clearing at the top of the bluff. Standing just inside the tree line, they stared at the scene before them. Hundreds of people dressed in dark clothing were assembled on the bluff. In the center of the bluff, a giant, black rock jutted out into the night sky like a huge, granite altar and Helga was pulling Hazel up onto it.

"There she is," Agnes cried. "We need to get her."

"Henry and I will go toward the top of the group," Rowan suggested. "You and Cat go toward the bottom. The first group that has an opportunity needs to go."

Agnes looked at her family and nodded her head. "Blessed be," she whispered a quiet blessing and then stepped forward into the crowd.

Henry and Rowan stepped back into the woods and continued farther up the path. Rowan reached for

Henry's hand and clasped it tightly. "She's going to be fine," she whispered to him. "Tell me that she's going to be fine."

Henry opened his mouth, then swallowed and tried again. "Yes," he finally said, his voice hoarse with fear. "Yes. She'll be fine."

Chapter Sixty-six

Joseph raced through the woods toward the Willoughby house and then ran to the barn where he'd left Hazel. The door was wide open, and his stomach tightened. She knew there was danger tonight. She wouldn't have left her goats unprotected.

He ran to the loft and then out to the balcony she'd created. It was empty. He looked out around the grounds. The Jeep was gone too. Had something happened to Hazel? Had there been an emergency? Did they have to rush her to the hospital?

He shook his head. No, no hospitals. Rowan and Henry would have helped her. What else would cause them to leave their house tonight?

A familiar buzzing sound pulled him away from the view and to the floor of the balcony. There in the corner was his cell phone buzzing as a call came through. He picked it up.

"They've got Hazel," Donovan said immediately.

"What?" Joseph exclaimed.

"Cat sent me a message," Donovan explained.
"They brought Hazel to the ceremony."

"Where's the ceremony?" Joseph asked.

"The bluff near the lake," Donovan replied.
"Hurry! It's almost midnight."

Joseph allowed the adrenaline from the anger and
the fear move through his system, and he felt his body
respond. His limbs trembled, and his muscles rippled as he
transformed. But this time he was in control. This time he
knew exactly what he wanted. "Hazel," he whispered as
his body made its final transformation. "Ha—" And then
her name was swallowed up by a howl.

He leapt from the balcony and dove back into the
woods. He lifted his nose in the air, found her scent, and
followed it. The trees along the path disappeared into a
dark blur as he pushed his body with superhuman strength
toward his destination.

Suddenly, he picked up the sounds of more beasts
running through the woods. He lifted his nose and

inhaled, and his lips parted, showing his glistening fangs. He lifted his head to the air and howled again. An answering howl echoed back.

He ran forward, through the trees towards a clearing, and the two paths merged. Now, instead of a lone alpha he was part of a pack. He glanced quickly over his shoulder as he ran, and his heart leapt with joy. The Wulffolk, in all their sizes and shapes, ran as wolf people behind him, allowing him to be their alpha, allowing him to take the lead. He nodded with satisfaction. The Wulffolk were on the hunt!

Chapter Sixty-seven

Hazel stood on the huge, black ledge and looked around the crowd, her stomach reeling and her knees weak. Helga yanked on her arms again, pulling her forward. Hazel turned and glared at her. If she got out of this, the first thing she was going to do was slap that bitch.

Mayor Bates climbed up next to them and put his hands up to silence the crowd.

This can't be good, Hazel thought.

"Tonight, during this blood moon, we come together to celebrate the Master," he yelled out. "We offer vows of fidelity to him, and we seal our vows with the blood of a virgin."

Hazel took a deep breath, forcing herself not to react and not to faint.

"Come," Mayor Bates continued. "Let us call to our leader. Master. Master. Master."

The crowd chanted with him, the chorus of "Master" echoing across the lake. Suddenly, a rift appeared and grew from the base of the rock, like a door had been opened to the world below. Glowing red embers shot from the rift, and Hazel could detect the distinct smell of sulfur.

Helga yanked Hazel, spinning her around and pulling her backwards, closer to the rift. Leaning forward, Hazel fought Helga, using everything she had to go in the other direction.

"This is where you belong, witch," Helga spat. "Burning in hell."

Hazel shook her head. "No!" she yelled. "No! Someone help me!"

Helga yanked again, and Hazel could feel the heat from the rift on her back.

"We make this offering to you, Master," Mayor Bates chanted. "A virgin to satisfy your appetite."

Helga yanked again, and Hazel could feel herself slipping. "No!" she screamed, and she fell sideways onto the rock, pulling Helga down with her. She tried to roll onto her back, but Helga held on to her. "You're not going anywhere, witch," she cried.

Hazel turned to look over her shoulder just as a huge pillar of molten lava spewed forth from the rift. Hazel froze in horror as the pillar wavered back in forth in the air above her, like a python hypnotizing its prey. It swung back and forth, slowly getting lower and lower. Then, in a flash of heat, it shot down and enveloped Helga in its flames. Before Helga could even scream, her face and her body were a pile of ash.

Hazel rolled over onto her back, gasping in shock. She moved and felt a lump underneath her. She looked to her side and saw that Helga's arm, up to her elbow, was still holding to the handcuffs. She screamed and rolled, the scorched arm flying through the air to land with a smack at the end of the rock.

Freed from the arm, Hazel scrambled backwards, using any purchase of her feet against the rock to get as far away from the rift as she could.

"Grab her!" Mayor Bates yelled, sliding towards her. "Somebody grab her!"

His demands were lost in the shouts of horror coming from the crowds below the rock. Hazel turned her head and looked out to see dozens of wolf people charging out of the woods towards the audience, their fangs bared, and their claws exposed. The rest of the coven stampeded towards the parking lot, knocking each other down in their mad rush to escape.

"Hazel, sweetheart, over here."

Hazel looked over and saw her mother at the edge of the rock. "Mom," she cried, sliding towards her.

"Not so fast," Mayor Bates said, lifting a large knife up over his head. "I will get my sacrifice."

Hazel screamed as the knife began its descent, but a blur of fur and teeth knocked Mayor Bates back onto the rock. Without looking back, Hazel slid the rest of the way down the rock face to her mother.

"Mom," she sobbed when her mother embraced her.

Her mother held her tight and rocked her. "It's okay, sweetheart," she soothed. "It's okay."

Chapter Sixty-eight

Joseph walked toward Mayor Bates, his claws clicking against the granite below, his lips drawn up in a vicious growl. He had watched the whole scene as he charged across the clearing, watched Helga yank Hazel towards the fiery pit, watched Hazel fight for her life and, finally, watched Bates in his last final attempt to kill the love of his life.

Hate, pure unadulterated hate, flowed through his veins. He could almost feel Bates' bones crunch beneath his claws. He could nearly taste Bates' blood on his fangs, and he could imagine the screams of terror as he ripped the little man's throat open from side to side. His feral eyes glowed with anger, and his fangs dripped with saliva as he cornered his prey.

The fire glowed brighter as Joseph closed in on Bates. Almost like a child clapping with glee, the fire bubbled and rolled as Joseph's hate grew. He reached out

425

his hand to grasp Bates' neck when the man was ripped away from him and tossed several feet away.

"You don't want to do that, Norwalk," Donovan said, coming up from behind him.

Joseph whirled around and growled at Donovan. "You!" he roared. "He's my kill."

"Do you hear what you're saying?" Donavan asked. "Do you understand what's happening to you?"

"Did you see what he did to Hazel?" Joseph yelled. "She was nearly killed!"

"Yes, I did!' Donovan screamed back. "And now I see what the Master is trying to do to you!"

Joseph stared at Donovan, his mouth slack. "What?" he asked, confusion more than anger in his voice.

"He's trying to use you," Donovan said gently. "Don't let him get hold of you too. Go over and hug Hazel. She needs you. He doesn't."

Slowly transforming from wolf to man, Joseph looked over to where Agnes was rocking Hazel in her arms. Then he looked back to Donovan and nodded. "Thank you," he said earnestly.

Donovan nodded back. "No problem."

Donovan watched Joseph walk across the rock face, then jump down next to Hazel and Agnes and put his hand on Hazel's shoulder. He saw the joy in Hazel's face as she leapt into Joseph's arms, and he wondered if Cat would ever look at him that way again.

He moved slowly across the rock face to Mayor Bates, laying in a quivering mass in a corner. "It's over, Mayor Bates," he said. "The Master has—"

Suddenly, the fiery pillar swooped over Donovan's shoulder and engulfed Mayor Bates. Jumping back, Donovan was shocked to see nothing left of the mayor but a narrow pile of ashes that slowly blew away in the wind.

"Donovan, listen to me."

Donovan stopped and looked around. There was no one there.

"Donovan, you can't see me with your eyes, but you can hear me in your mind," the voice said. "I have been watching you, and I like what I see. I would like you to be my commander."

Donovan felt his heart pound in his chest. Was it fear or excitement?

I can do this, he thought. I can get close and help destroy him from the inside.

Donovan walked over to the rift and looked down at the churning lava. "Yes, Master, I am yours to command," he said.

Cat froze, her hand only inches away from Donovan's shoulder, and her eyes widened as she heard his words. Biting back a tearful sob, she stepped backwards away from the man she'd once loved.

Chapter Sixty-nine

Hazel sat on a love seat wrapped in a blanket and Joseph's arms. Agnes brought her a cup of tea. "How are you feeling, sweetheart?" Agnes asked.

"Much better," Hazel said. "Thank you, Mom."

Joseph leaned forward and kissed her head, wrapping his arms even more securely around her. She looked up at him and laughed. "I'm not going anywhere," she teased.

He looked down at her. "No," he said. "You're not. And neither am I."

Her eyes filled with tears, and she lifted a hand and stroked his chin. "I'm so glad," she whispered. "So very glad."

"You did it," he told her. "You saved me."

"How?" she asked.

"I heard your heart," he replied. "I heard the echo of your heart against mine when I was running, and I remembered the last time I'd heard it. And then I remembered you."

He kissed her tenderly and then lifted his head. "I should have known I could never forget you," he said.

"What I want to know," Henry said, and then he turned to Hazel. "And I don't mean this the way it's going to sound. But, why did the Mas...I mean, the mosquito choose Helga?"

Hazel nodded. "I agree," she said. "I mean, I'm really glad he did, but, yeah, why?"

Rowan glanced over at Agnes, and Agnes nodded.

"Okay you two," Hazel said. "No secrets. What's up?"

"Well, actually, it's our fault," Rowan said. "Henry's and mine."

"What?" Henry asked, sitting up and looking at Rowan. "What did I do?"

"When we did the DNA transfer, we didn't think of all of the possible ramifications," she answered. "And when we created the spells, we didn't think about what our words could mean other than what we thought we meant."

"What? What did our words mean?" Henry asked.

Then he repeated the words from the spell.

"To heal a wound that lies deep inside,

We ask for power to be astral guides.

Two becomes one, resolve and remedy.

 Life is renewed, so mote it be."

He turned to Rowan and smiled. "No," he said. "Really?"

She nodded. "I checked," she replied. "Really!"

He laughed delightedly. "That's wonderful," he said, smiling at Hazel and Joseph. "I mean that's really wonderful."

Hazel looked at Henry and then at Rowan. "What?" she asked. "What's so wonderful?"

"The Master didn't choose you because he needed a virgin," Rowan said.

"Wait!" both Joseph and Hazel protested.

"Which, you still are, technically," Henry inserted. "But when you and Joseph merged."

"And our spell included two becoming one and life being renewed," Rowan asked.

"And then, when you were so sick," Agnes added.

"I'm still lost," Hazel said. "What are we talking about here?"

Rowan stood up, walked over to her sister and placed her hands on her shoulders. "You're pregnant," she said.

"What?" Hazel stammered, placing her hands on her abdomen. "But I can't…"

"I looked," Rowan said. "Mom asked me to look because she felt an extra spirit when she hugged you."

"But, even it's that true, the baby is still too little," Hazel argued.

"I accelerated its growth," Rowan said. "When I accelerated the DNA process."

Hazel looked up to see Joseph gazing at her in wonder. "Joseph?" she asked quietly.

432

He stood, lifted her in his arms, stepped around all of the rest of people in the room and carried her outside to the deck. He gently placed her on a chair and then knelt before her, taking her hands in his own.

"I adore you," he said, kissing the palms of her hands. "And this baby is a miracle."

Then he reached up and kissed her lips. "You are a miracle."

She moved their entwined hands and laid them on her belly. "We are a miracle," she said softly. "And I'm so relieved I'm not going to have a puppy."

With a soft growl, he scooped her out of the chair, pulled her down into his lap, and kissed her until they were both breathless.

"My heart," he whispered, kissing her once again. "My only heart."

The End

About the author: Terri Reid lives near Freeport, the home of the Mary O'Reilly Mystery Series, and loves a good ghost story. An independent author, Reid uploaded her first book "Loose Ends – A Mary O'Reilly Paranormal Mystery" in August 2010. By the end of 2013, "Loose Ends" had sold over 200,000 copies. She has sixteen other books in the Mary O'Reilly Series, the first books in the following series - "The Blackwood Files," "The Order of Brigid's Cross," and "The Legend of the Horsemen." She also has a stand-alone romance, "Bearly in Love." Reid has enjoyed Top Rated and Hot New Release status in the Women Sleuths and Paranormal Romance category through Amazon US. Her books have been translated into Spanish, Portuguese and German and are also now also available in print and audio versions. Reid has been quoted in several books about the self-publishing industry including "Let's Get Digital" by David Gaughran and "Interviews with Indie Authors: Top Tips from Successful Self-Published Authors" by Claire

434

and Tim Ridgway. She was also honored to have some of her works included in A. J. Abbiati's book "The NORTAV Method for Writers – The Secrets to Constructing Prose Like the Pros."

She loves hearing from her readers at author@terrireid.com

Other Books by Terri Reid:

Mary O'Reilly Paranormal Mystery Series:
Loose Ends (Book One)

Good Tidings (Book Two)

Never Forgotten (Book Three)

Final Call (Book Four)

Darkness Exposed (Book Five)

Natural Reaction (Book Six)

Secret Hollows (Book Seven)

Broken Promises (Book Eight)

Twisted Paths (Book Nine)

Veiled Passages (Book Ten)

Bumpy Roads (Book Eleven)

Treasured Legacies (Book Twelve)

Buried Innocence (Book Thirteen)

Stolen Dreams (Book Fourteen)

Haunted Tales (Book Fifteen)

Deadly Circumstances (Book Sixteen)

Frayed Edges (Book Seventeen)

Delayed Departures (Book Eighteen)

Old Acquaintance (Book Nineteen)

Clear Expectations (Book Twenty)

Finders Mansion Mystery Series
Maybelle's Secret

Mary O'Reilly Short Stories

The Three Wise Guides

Tales Around the Jack O'Lantern 1

Tales Around the Jack O'Lantern 2

Tales Around the Jack O'Lantern 3

Auld Lang Syne

The Order of Brigid's Cross (Sean's Story)

The Wild Hunt (Book 1)

The Faery Portal (Book 2)

The Blackwood Files (Art's Story)

File One: Family Secrets

File Two: Private Wars

PRCD Case Files: The Ghosts Of New
Orleans -A Paranormal Research and Containment
Division Case File

Eochaidh: Legend of the Horseman (Book One)

Eochaidh: Legend of the Horsemen (Book Two)

Sweet Romances

Bearly in Love

Sneakers – A Swift Romance

Lethal Distraction – A Pierogies & Pumps Mystery

Novella

The Willoughby Witches

Rowan's Responsibility

Made in the USA
Lexington, KY
13 January 2019